Tides
&Drift

Tides & Drift

ADRIENNE YOUNG

TITAN BOOKS

Tides & Drift
Print edition ISBN: 9781803369471
E-book edition ISBN: 9781803369488

Published by Titan Books
A division of Titan Publishing Group Ltd
144 Southwark Street, London SE1 0UP
www.titanbooks.com

First Titan edition: February 2024
10 9 8 7 6 5 4 3 2 1

A CIP catalogue record for this title is available from
the British Library.

Printed and bound by CPI Group (UK) Ltd, Croydon CR0 4YY.

CONTENTS

INTRODUCTION

The first time I ever visited the Narrows was the day *Fable* first came to me. I often get story ideas in a single picture. I then spend months, sometimes years, answering the who, what, when, where, why, and how of that picture before I start writing it. With *Fable*, it was a girl standing on a beach, watching a ship sail away. Little did I know that she was on the island of Jeval in a place called the Narrows, a little forgotten corner of The Unnamed Sea.

In the book *Fable*, we follow Fable on her quest across the Narrows to find her father and claim her place on his crew. After narrowly escaping the retribution of a dangerous dredger named Koy, she is forced to trust West, a young trader who will steal her heart, as will his crew. Willa, Paj, Auster and Hamish become the family Fable never had as she carves out her own stake in the world.

In *Namesake*, Fable and West's journey takes them to Bastian, a glittering city in the Unnamed Sea where Fable's mother's past and Fable's role within it are revealed. When her path unexpectedly crosses with Koy once again, she finds they have more in common than she thought. We also learn more about Auster's mysterious background when we meet the Roths, the crime family he left behind when he fell in love with Paj. And in the end, with a new future at the tip of their fingers, Willa decides to make her own fate by leaving the crew behind.

Back in Bastian, Henrik, the patriarch of the Roths summons home his long-lost niece, Bryn, in *The Last Legacy*. The fate of the Roths as a family takes a turn, shifting their ties forever, but all of these stories find their origins in *Saint*, the tale of Fable's father as a young dreamer at the dawn of the Narrows and the earth-shattering love he shared with her mother, Isolde.

Now, I am happy to give you *Tides* and *Drift*, two Narrows novellas that give you a peek into the stories that bridge the gap between these characters and their futures in this world. *Tides* follows the origin love story between Paj and Auster before the events of *Fable*, as they defy the Roths definitions of family, loyalty, and faith. In *Drift*, we follow Willa and Koy after the events of *Namesake*, as they set out to open their own port on the island of Jeval.

I hope you love wandering this world with these characters as much as I do. I can't wait to see where they go next.

TIMELINE OF BOOKS

Saint

Tides

Fable

Namesake

The Last Legacy

Drift

TIDES

ONE

The harbor was dead, and that was never a good sign.

I leaned against the wall of the merchant's house beside Murrow, my eyes trained on the ship anchored in the fourth bay down the docks. The *Scourge* was a midsized schooner with three masts and a crew that was short at least a few hands. It arrived in Bastian every two weeks like clockwork and dropped anchor for a single night on its way to Nimsmire. We'd been watching it for months, checking the quantities unloaded against the harbor master's logs.

I pulled my pocket watch from my vest. It clicked, opening in my palm. The yellow light of the streetlamp gleamed on the glass as I tilted it. "Two minutes," I murmured, looking over my shoulder to Murrow.

My cousin's curling brown hair was barely contained beneath his cap. It was his attempt at being inconspicuous, but there was nothing ordinary about him. He was uncommonly tall and lanky like his father, with huge feet, and his pants were almost always too short—a detail that aggravated our uncle

Henrik to no end. He liked the family to be clean-shaven, buttoned-up, and shined like a brass buckle, even if we were doing the work of sea urchins.

Behind him, Ezra nodded in answer, a look of utter boredom on his angled face. His features were distinctly *not* Roth, though in the years since Henrik plucked him out of a rival's workshop and brought him home, he'd managed to end up looking like us in other ways. His nearly black hair was combed back, the collar of his jacket flipped up against the wind. It wasn't often he ventured out of the workshop, but I needed three bodies for this job if I was going to pull it off. My uncle didn't like mistakes.

The *Scourge*'s route stretched all the way to the Narrows and carried everything from silk to salted pork, but it was one of the few Bastian-based trading operations that had license to carry the thing we were after—Sowan rye. The potent spirit was made in sea brine barrels by crofters in the north, and there wasn't a bastard in Bastian who wouldn't pay top coin for the stuff. That was exactly what my uncle Henrik was counting on.

The harbor bell rang, signaling the official close of business in the merchant's house, but most of the ship crews were already drinking in the city's taverns. That should have been my first clue. Things were never that easy.

I snapped the watch closed and tucked it back into the pocket against my ribs. "Let's go."

Murrow pushed off the wall and stepped out first, shoving his hands into his pockets and starting up the main dock. He kept his face down, turning it just enough to keep it from catching the light of the streetlamps. It was more instinct than anything. We'd learned to be invisible at a young age, when his father and our uncles started using us as decoys. *Might as well make use of them*, Henrik had said. It had been the same for him. No one looked twice at a well-dressed boy in a tailored jacket. Not unless they could see the Roth tattoo on your arm. I'd been given that when I was twelve, like everyone else in the family.

Ezra ran a hand through his hair, slicking it back from his face as we waited. Murrow passed the second bay, then the third. There wasn't so much as a hitch in his gait as he reached the fourth. He waited until he passed a stack of barrels, and when he was illuminated in the pool of light from the next streetlamp, he took one hand from his pocket and let it fall to his side. That was the signal.

It was clear.

I didn't hesitate, moving up the dock with Ezra on my heels. The harbor was patrolled by the watch, and there would be at least one member from the *Scourge*'s crew guarding the unloaded inventory waiting for delivery to the merchant's house. But the pickup wasn't coming. I'd made sure of that. And more often than not, the crew member left to guard the cargo was half drunk by this hour.

Moonlight rippled on the surface of the calm, black sea to our left, and the elevated street stretched out along the water to our right. I watched Ezra's shadow from the corner of my eye, counting the steps. They were like a heartbeat, steady and even until we reached the *Scourge,* and as soon as the dock broke off I turned sharply, disappearing between the barrels. Ezra took the next opening, and I listened to his footsteps on the other side of the cargo as we both made our way toward the crates we were looking for.

I searched the lids until I spotted a stack burned with the port seal of Sowan. A relieved breath escaped my lips and I knocked on one of them with a fist, letting Ezra know I'd found it. A soft splash sounded below the slats of the dock under my feet, and I looked down to see a near-invisible Murrow pulling a pair of oars from the water. He stood, catching hold of the dock with both hands to hold a small rowboat in place.

I hoisted the first box into my arms, careful not to jostle the corked bottles inside. Ezra was already climbing into the boat below and as soon as his boots hit the hull, he reached up, ready to take the crate from me. I squatted onto my haunches, leaning out over the water. But I froze when the prick of sharp metal stung against the side of my neck, just below my jaw. A chill ran down my spine and the crate almost slipped through my fingers. I'd had a knife to my throat enough times to know what a blade felt like.

"Stand up." A deep voice sounded in the dark behind me, and I set the crate down between my feet. I lifted my hands slowly out to the side as I rose.

Below, Murrow stared up at me with wide eyes. Ezra was pulling the knife from his belt. But by the time they made it back onto the dock, I'd be bleeding. One shout into the night air for the harbor watch and all three of us would go down.

The moment Murrow began to hoist himself from the

boat, I kicked my boot to the side in a quick sweep, knocking his grip from the dock. He tumbled back into the hull with a crash, and one of the oars slipped into the water, disappearing. He cursed, trying to leap back up for the dock, but it was too late. The current was already tugging the boat out into the bay, the dark swallowing it whole.

"Turn around." The voice spoke again with the same patient cadence.

I obeyed, turning my back to the ship, and when I saw the face before me, my eyes narrowed. The trader was young, probably my age. A deckhand working his way up the ranks of the crew.

He looked down at me with a flat expression, his black eyes like polished pieces of onyx. They were as dark as his skin, but as he took a step closer to me, the light from the streetlamp shimmered over it like the smooth face of a black pearl.

"Willing to die for your helmsman's coffers?" I muttered, glaring at him.

"I don't give a shit about his ledgers, but you touch that rye and it's coming out of *my* coin." He lifted the knife, forcing me to raise my chin. "So if you want it, you'll have to find a way to cut me first."

There was no way for me to reach my own knife quick enough, and he knew it. Any minute, the watch would come across those crates on their rounds, and then they'd be hauling me up to the merchant's house. That was if I were lucky. It was more likely that this deckhand would let his helmsman deal with me, and that would be worse. Much worse.

17

His gaze drifted to my left hand. "Pull up your sleeve."

I stood up straighter, trying to read the look in his eye. He wasn't stupid, and that wouldn't bode well for me either. I reached for the cuff of my right sleeve instead and unbuttoned it, taking my time.

"Not that one," his voice grated.

I grinned, and he looked surprised by it, leaning back away from me slightly. His eyes didn't leave mine until I had the sleeve rolled up to the elbow, and he took hold of my wrist roughly, pulling my arm into the light between us. He glanced at the tattoo on the inside of my forearm: two entwined snakes eating one another's tails. The ouroboros was the mark that every member of my family had. The mark of the Roths.

His eyes lifted again, running over my face slowly, as if he were trying to solve some puzzle he saw there. His fingers tightened around my wrist, and when boots sounded on the other side of the slip, he suddenly let me go. I glanced at the darkness behind him as two shadows appeared on the dock. The harbor watch.

Any other trader would have called out to them or used their knife by now, especially after seeing my tattoo, but he stayed quiet. The boots moved closer, reaching the next slip, and I tried not to think about what my uncle would do when he had to come haul me out of the merchant's house.

As soon as I thought it, the prick of his blade at my throat vanished. The moonlight flashed on the steel between us before the trader slipped it back into his belt.

My brow furrowed as I looked up into his face, and for a moment, I could have sworn I saw a smirk playing on his lips. But before I could open my mouth to speak, he shoved me hard in the chest with both hands and I flew back, the heels of my boots scraping on the wood slats as I fell from the dock.

I hit the cold seawater and plunged beneath it, thrashing as my jacket tangled and the bubbles spilled from my lips. My shoulder hit one of the pillars holding up the dock as the current swept around me, and when I saw the moonlight above I swam toward it, the weight of my boots heavy beneath me. By the time I broke the surface with a gasp, I was already out from under the docks, being pulled into the bay.

I flung my wet hair back, blinking furiously as I turned, trying to see in the dark. In the distance, a silhouette stood on the docks, only half lit by the string of streetlamps behind him. He watched me drift away from the harbor, and as I swallowed another ragged breath, he disappeared.

TWO

A bruised cheek was nothing to the punishments I'd seen my uncle Henrik dole out over my lifetime. He hadn't said a word when I showed up in his study that night in my ruined suit and told him what happened to the crates of Sowan rye. He'd simply set down his smoking pipe and stood from his desk before striking me across the cheek with a closed fist. Then he'd told me I'd have to pay for the handwoven rug I'd ruined with the seawater still dripping from me.

In the two weeks since I'd botched the job at the docks, the mark on my face had faded, but the consequences were far from over. Henrik had me manning the most dreaded post he had to assign—the tavern. I'd spent morning to night sitting on the stool at the end of the counter over a bottle of rye while Ezra ran my pickup routes in the city. He hadn't been happy about the new arrangement either, forced to leave his work at the forge to cover my jobs. And Murrow was even more irritated. I'd broken two of his fingers when I kicked

20

his hands from the dock, but I'd seen no sense in risking all three of our necks. Not when the job had been mine in the first place.

The post at the tavern, however dull, was a simple one. Taverns were a thoroughfare for the traders stopping in Bastian on their routes, and it was the best place to collect information. There was no one more loose-lipped than the low-level crew members of a trading outfit, using their one night on land to fill themselves with rye before they set sail again. The stool at the end of the bar was bought and paid for by Henrik and was reserved for the person on the lowest rung of his favor. Ever since the night at the docks, that was me.

I'd been sitting at that counter for twelve days straight, staring into a rye glass and keeping a mental register of slurred, broken conversations. Every night, I wrote them down in a report for Henrik, and when I climbed into bed, I still smelled like the sour rags the barkeep used to clean the counter. The next morning, I put on a clean shirt and went back.

When I asked Henrik how long he planned to keep me there, he'd just laughed at me. I couldn't help but think I deserved it. I'd done a shit job of accounting for the crew member on the docks, assuming that whoever it was would be just like the fools that filled the tavern. The mistake could have gotten me killed. Worse, it could have gotten Ezra and Murrow killed.

I turned the glass on the counter, pinching my eyes closed to quell the throbbing in my head. The dim light of the oil lamps cast everything in a grimy glow, and as the moon rose, so did the noise. Throngs of trading crews spilled into the tavern until it was filled to the brim, bringing the smell of stinking bodies and spilled rye. The barkeep's daughters wedged themselves through the crush of people with their pitchers in the air, refilling the glasses on the rickety tables.

I tipped my head to one side, stretching my stiff neck. There hadn't been a scrap of news in days that Henrik would find interesting, but I wasn't allowed to leave the stool until half past eleven. If I did, my uncle would know. Somehow, he always knew.

I tugged at the chain of my pocket watch until it fell from my vest, then caught it in my hand as a man sat down beside me. The smooth silver casing had been cast by Ezra, and my name was engraved on the inside. I set it onto the counter, staring at its glass face. Still more than an hour to go.

The air was stifling, and sweat dripped down my back, soaking my vest. I sighed with relief when the doors to the street opened again and a gust of damp, cold air rushed into the tavern. It tingled against my hot skin and though Henrik wouldn't approve, I unbuttoned the top of my shirt, pulling it open at the throat.

Someone tapped the counter a few stools down, signaling the barkeep, and I rubbed at my temples, groaning.

"Three."

I stilled when I heard the voice. Deep and rhythmic. It was one I recognized.

Down the bar, a hand was splayed on the wood countertop. Smooth, obsidian skin. I leaned forward, just enough to see

TIDES & DRIFT

his face. It was the trader from the *Scourge*. The one who'd held a blade to my throat and then pushed me into the water.

The barkeep pulled three green glasses from the shelf behind him, and the trader propped himself on his elbows as he waited, tapping his fingers. He watched as the glasses were filled, but when he reached into his pocket for the coin to pay, I silently lifted two fingers from the counter. The barkeep answered with a nod, dismissing him.

"No need," the barkeep murmured, moving to the next person waiting.

The trader stared at him, confused, before he turned and searched the bar with a frown. He went rigid when his eyes landed on me, and I picked up my bottle of rye, refilling my own glass.

"Move." I flicked a hand toward the man sitting beside me and he instantly stood, scrambling clumsily out of the way.

If the trader thought I was going to offer more of an invitation than that, then he was mistaken. But he seemed to consider whether he wanted to take the seat, glancing around the tavern. There wasn't a single chair left in the house.

He finally picked up his rye and set the glasses beside me, sliding onto the stool. He took a single sharp sip before he drained the glass in one swallow and lined it up neatly beside the other two.

"I suppose you expect me to thank you," he muttered, not looking at me.

I tried not to smile, turning my glass in a circle on the bar again. There was something strange about the way he spoke.

I'd noticed it that night. He folded his arms on the counter and I watched the travel of light across his skin from the corner of my eye. It was that same shimmer I'd seen on the docks.

"You just came from Dern?" I asked, taking the shot of rye.

He looked suspicious now, studying me. "How do you know that?"

I shrugged. "I know everything about that ship. I was working that job for months before you—"

"Saved your life?" he finished, arching one eyebrow.

I did smile at that. It was true. His helmsman probably would have strung me up from the mast if he'd turned me in. Even the harbor watch might have found reason to make sure I disappeared, depending on their mood or the current state of their relationship with my uncles.

"I suppose you expect me to thank you." I repeated his words back to him.

The line of his mouth tilted and he stifled a laugh. Whatever he was thinking, he didn't say it.

"I'm Auster," I said, turning on the stool to face him. I held out a hand between us.

He twisted to stare at it silently for a moment before he sat up straight. "Paj." He took my hand and shook it, his eyes running over my clothes. "I see you had that fancy jacket cleaned."

"Replaced." I grinned. "Cost me a purse of copper."

"Serves you right." He picked up his second glass.

I liked this bastard. "You're from Bastian." I meant it as a question, but it didn't sound like one. "What part?"

Paj went stiff again. "Why?"

Heat came into my cheeks when I realized that I didn't know why. I just wanted to talk to him. "No reason." I refilled my glass, though my head was already swimming. Maybe that was what was wrong with me.

He cleared his throat. "North End. I was born in North End."

I was surprised that he'd answered, and even more surprised that he'd answered honestly. I knew how listen for a lie like I knew how to do the figures in my uncle's ledger.

"What about you?" he asked.

I closed the pocket watch on the bar, suddenly unconcerned with the time. "Lower Vale." I gave him the answer easily, watching his face for whatever reaction might surface there. But there was none.

"That's right," he said, almost to himself. "That's where all the Roths are born."

Anyone from Bastian had heard the name and the stories that came with it. But the only people who knew which of those stories were true were the ones who had the ouroboros tattooed on their arm.

He reached for the third glass. I searched for something else to say when the thought crossed my mind that once he finished, he might get up and leave. I was even more unsettled to find that I didn't want him to.

But as soon as I thought it, the doors to the street flung open again and the night air poured back inside. I looked over my shoulder to see Murrow pushing into the tavern.

His broken fingers were still wrapped together, and his hand swung heavily at his side as he made his way toward me.

I let out a breath, clenching my teeth. When I looked back to Paj, he was eyeing me inquisitively.

The crowd parted as Murrow stalked toward the bar, and when he reached me, he picked up my glass and dumped the rye into his mouth. He slammed it onto the counter as he swallowed it down. "Time to go."

Paj looked between us, an unspoken question in his eyes. His last glass of rye was still in his hand, dangling from his fingertips.

I cleared my throat, tucking the watch back into my vest. Then I raked both hands through my hair to slick it back before I slid off the stool and pushed the unfinished bottle of rye toward Paj. He looked up, his eyes meeting mine for just a moment. Just long enough to make a tingle wake on my skin.

As soon as I felt it, I turned on my heel, pushing into the crowd gathered around the bar. Murrow followed, and I didn't look back, pinning my eyes to the floor.

Murrow jerked the door open. "Who was that?" The question was halfhearted, and I was glad. That meant he hadn't recognized him.

I pulled up the collar of my jacket before I stepped out into the wind. "No one."

‹▼›

THREE

‹▲›

Of all the reckless things I'd done, *this* was by far the stupidest.

I paced the walkway at the top of the stairs that overlooked the docks, fidgeting with the chain of my pocket watch and resisting the urge to look at the horizon. Every time the harbor master's eyes landed on me, he looked nervous. But for once, I wasn't there to do my uncle's bidding. By some twist of seriously misguided fate, I was waiting for the *Scourge*.

It had been two weeks since I'd seen Paj at the tavern and every single day since had been measured by the number of hours until his ship would dock again. It was immediately followed by whether he'd come back to the tavern, but I found as the day drew on that I didn't want to take the chance that he wouldn't.

I'd changed my mind more than once. In fact, I'd barely slept the night before the *Scourge* was due in Bastian, tossing and turning in the moonlight cast through my window. But somehow, I'd found myself standing in the harbor before the sun set, and though I was more convinced with every passing minute that I'd made a huge mistake, I couldn't bring myself to leave.

The bell rang once, signaling a ship to port, and my chest grew tight as I finally looked out to the water. The dark wood of the schooner was a dead giveaway, even before I saw the crest of the *Scourge* on the sail. An overwhelming desire to turn and walk back up the steps to the street gripped me, a stone sinking in my stomach.

Henrik had released me from my sentence at the tavern days before, and tonight my uncles thought I was keeping an eye on a gem merchant who'd recently acquired a new cache of rare emeralds. It hadn't occurred to me until that moment what would happen if they caught me. If anyone asked questions, Murrow would cover for me. So would Ezra. But Henrik had a nose for lying like he had a nose for gems. And that thought unnerved me.

A line of dockworkers directed the *Scourge* into the slip and I shifted on my feet, studying the ship's deck. There was no sign of Paj, and if I left now, I'd save myself the embarrassment of whatever he'd say when he saw me standing there. But for a reason I couldn't quite put together, my boots stayed planted on the dock as the heaving lines were tied and the anchor splashed into the water.

My heart beat unevenly behind my ribs as the crew started the climb down the ladder, and I rubbed my cleanly shaven face with the butt of my hand. What the hell was I doing there?

I turned my back to the slip, watching the steps ahead with

my finger wound so tight in the chain of my watch that it bit into my skin.

"Auster?"

I whirled, swallowing hard when I saw him.

Paj stood at the bottom of the stairs, looking up at me with a satchel flung over his shoulder and his hand hooked into the strap. He looked utterly confused, and I immediately regretted each and every moment that had led me to the harbor.

He glanced up and down the dock before his eyes traveled back to me again. "What are you doing here?"

My mouth opened, a thousand muddled words flitting through my mind, but not a single one found my lips.

Paj's eyes narrowed in a kind of amusement. Like he enjoyed whatever ridiculous expression was cast over my face. "Were you *waiting* for me?"

The overwhelming humiliation of it was like being skinned alive. Right there, in front of everyone on the docks. "Maybe." There was no use it lying. I already looked like an idiot.

He stared at me as his crewmates filed around him, coming up the stairs and shouldering past us. It took a few moments for Paj to finally climb the steps, and when he was standing on the one below mine, he stared up into my face. "You hungry?"

Yes, this was *enormously* stupid. But I didn't care. "Yeah," I answered.

"All right." He stepped around me and I watched him go up the stairs before I followed.

When we reached the busy street, Paj kept walking, making

turn after turn without looking back. I couldn't help but glance up to the windows of the buildings around us and take note of who was standing on the corners. My uncle had eyes everywhere and only one of them needed to find me in order to land me in trouble.

But Paj moved with an ease through the city, his shoulders drawn down his back and his eyes straight ahead. It made me anxious. I was sure I'd never looked like that. Not ever.

He was taking us to North End. I'd known by the accent that he hadn't grown up in Bastian, and it was no surprise. Most traders starting at the bottom of crews hailed from North End or Lower Vale.

We reached a small door set into a wall lined with framed windows, and Paj had to duck beneath the doorframe because he was too tall for it. When I closed it behind us, the woman inside lit up, her eyes bright. "Hey, honey."

She was an older, chipper woman with hair piled on top of her head in a knot and an apron tied around her waist. Her smile faltered just a little when her eyes landed on me, and I looked down to my clothes, cursing myself. I could have at least at the sense to leave my jacket. No one in this part of town dressed like this, and all I needed was for rumors of a Roth wandering around North End to get back to my uncles.

Paj dropped his satchel on the ground and pulled a small chair from the wooden ledge that ran along the windows, taking a seat. When I realized he was waiting for me to do the same, I unbuttoned my jacket and let it slide from my shoulders. I draped it over the chair beside him before I sat.

"So?" Paj said, setting one elbow onto the ledge. His face was illuminated on one side by the light coming through the window, and I studied the angle of his cheek, holding my breath. I'd wondered over the last two weeks if the haze of the rye had exaggerated my memory, because I had never seen anyone as strikingly beautiful as he was.

"So, what?" I managed.

"Why were you waiting for me at the docks?"

I didn't know if he was trying to embarrass me or if he genuinely wanted to know. His face gave away nothing.

"I don't really know," I admitted.

To my surprise, that seemed to be enough of an answer for him. He didn't press.

"What will it be, Paj?" The woman called from the other side of the little room, where she was folding squares of grey linen.

He leaned back in the chair to look at her. "Whatever you're cooking."

"And for the pretty one?" She eyed me.

"Same," he answered. "And tea."

I couldn't identify the smell coming from the kitchen, but the place was just a tiny stall with a few tables. It looked like one of the soup houses in Lower Vale that was filled with the same people each day.

My chair creaked as I leaned forward, looking down the street again to get a view of each corner.

"What are you doing?" Paj asked, watching me.

"Nothing."

31

"You look like you're looking for someone."

I shook my head, giving an easy smile out of habit. It was one of the first things I'd learned as a Roth. Charm covered a multitude of sins.

Two steaming bowls of stewed turnips and cuts of meat landed on the window ledge, followed by two cups of tea. Paj thanked the woman, picking up the slice of thick bread that was wedged on the dish below.

He shoveled a bite into his mouth while I reached into my pocket for my purse. I opened it and dumped several coppers into my palm before Paj reached out, setting a hand on top of them. He kept it there while the woman waited for him to fish four coins from his own jacket.

He smiled at her as he dropped them into her hand, and she looked between us before she walked back to the counter.

"Don't do that." He let go of me, leaving behind the burn of his skin on mine.

"What?"

"Throw coin around." He tore the bread in two. "You're not in Lower Vale."

I watched the woman, tucking the purse back into my vest. Her hands were focused on the linens, but every few breaths, she glanced at me. "Seemed like she was a friend," I said lowly, picking up my teacup.

"Mine. Not yours." He dipped the bread into the stew.

I sipped from the cup, eyeing the way the muscle in his jaw moved under the skin as he chewed. But I couldn't bring myself to pick up my spoon.

"How'd you end up on the *Scourge*?" I asked.

He lifted an eyebrow, studying me. "Same way anyone ends up on a crew. Needed a wage and was willing to drown for it."

"Dangerous work on a ship."

"Honest, though." There was another meaning in his words, and I didn't miss them. "I'm sure it's no more dangerous than work with the Roths."

I bit the inside of my cheek and instinctively straightened the cuffs of my shirt. It was as if the tattoo on my arm was burning a hole in my skin.

"Am I right?"

"I don't want to talk about my family," I said, a little more gruffly than I meant to.

He measured me for a moment, tearing the bread again. "All right."

He finished eating without another word and I picked at the stew, my stomach in knots. The tea was cold by the time I finished it, and Paj took his time, watching the people on the street pass the window until it was dark. The silence didn't bother me. In fact, I liked it. The house I lived in with my family was always loud. There were always people coming and going, and I never slept well because the windows rattled at night.

It was strange to be outside of my family's realm. It was strange to be sitting so close to someone who wasn't one of us.

"Ready?"

I blinked, turning to look at Paj. He leaned into the ledge, letting his eyes meet mine.

"Sure," I answered.

He dropped the satchel over his shoulder as he stood. I left the half-eaten stew behind, following him back outside. We walked the street in the dark and I avoided the streetlamps, dodging the circles of light on the ground and keeping a watch on the rooftops.

The air blowing in from the sea was cool and clean, and every time we reached the top of a hill, the view of the city below appeared like a twinkling blanket. Paj didn't talk and I didn't ask any more questions. It wasn't fair to expect answers if I wasn't going to give him any in return, but I found that I didn't mind that either. Walking in the quiet darkness made me feel like we were invisible.

It wasn't until more than an hour had gone by that I realized we weren't walking back to the harbor. We were just . . . walking. Up to the center of the city and then west toward the Merchant's District. When we got to the piers along the southern shore, we stood on the rocky outcropping over the water and watched the harbor, talking about nothing. He told me about the different types of ships he'd worked on and about the time he'd been left behind by accident and had to find a way back to Bastian. He talked about the Narrows and the color of the water there and the tools the navigator used on the ship. He talked until the faintest glow of sunrise was painting the sky.

That was when Paj finally started walking back toward the harbor, and I reluctantly followed, the pit in my stomach growing heavier with every step. When we reached the archway that opened to the docks, he fell silent again, and I came down the steps behind him, my cold hands finding my pockets.

He watched the *Scourge* over my shoulder. It loomed over us like a giant in the dark.

"I've never been on a ship," I said, half laughing. It felt like the first thing I'd spoken in hours. "Not a moving one, anyway." I'd snuck onto plenty of anchored vessels to steal cargo, but I'd never sailed. In fact, the idea of being on open water made my skin crawl.

He smiled incredulously as if he didn't believe me, but his look slowly turned curious. "You're serious?"

I shrugged. "Yeah."

Paj stared at me and his brow wrinkled in a way that made him impossibly more handsome. Like he was really thinking hard about something. Trying to work something out. He took a step toward me suddenly, and before I knew what he was doing, he was so close that I could smell the sea on him. Like wind and water.

He looked at me for a moment before his mouth pressed to mine, and a feeling like the whole of the sky filling my chest made the air in my lungs ache. His hand gently slid around my neck as he kissed me, putting the taste of salt on my tongue. As quickly as he'd done it, he was suddenly gone, breaking away from me and putting inches of air between us.

I stared at him wordlessly, my eyes searching his until a soft smile broke on his lips. In the next breath, he turned on his heel, leaving me standing in the dark.

FOUR

Two weeks felt like two years.

I kept busy with anything and everything my uncle asked of me, doing the pickup rounds and fetching deliveries. I even volunteered to take the tavern shift for two days to pass the time until the *Scourge* came back to Bastian.

I'd nearly convinced myself that the night I'd spent walking the streets of the city with Paj hadn't happened. That it was one of my sleepless nights turned into a waking dream. That's what it had felt like.

I sat at the desk in front of the window in my room after family dinner, working the sums of the ledger for a third time because Henrik liked them done in threes. Always threes. The numbers blurred together on the page under my hand and I scratched the quill on the parchment, counting in my head until the sound of tapping finally got my attention. Three seabirds were pecking at the glass, their gleaming eyes watching me.

I sighed, taking the last piece of bread from the plate at

the corner of the desk and crushing it in my hand until it was broken into crumbs. Then I unlatched the window and let it swing open on the rusted hinges. The birds fluttered off the ledge as I set down the plate, then came back, pecking at the pieces until they were gone.

In the distance, the sun was still hovering well over the horizon. I groaned, setting my forehead against the windowsill. There were still at least a few hours before sundown.

I forced myself back to the desk and crumpled the parchment I was working on, starting the count over. My uncles' voices boomed downstairs as they checked and sorted gems in the workshop over a bottle of rye. It was a comforting sound. The three of them had been the only fathers I'd ever known. My own father was their cousin, and he was lost at sea before any memory I could recall. Not long after, my grandmother had taken up residence in Nimsmire, leaving me to be raised by Henrik and the others. That was the way of things in this family. We all belonged to each other.

Even though we all lived in the house, family dinners were usually the only time every member of the family was in the same room. Once a week, we gathered around the long table in the dining room, and Sylvie, the kitchen maid, lit the candles on the chandelier before she set each place with porcelain and silver. That night, I'd spent the entire time watching the sun out the window, waiting for it to fall.

I tapped the tip of the quill nervously against the desk, trying to focus, but the only thing I had thought about in fourteen days was Paj and the explosion that had ignited in my chest when he kissed me. And every time the memory breathed back to life, so did the sinking feeling in my gut.

I set a finger on the first line of numbers, starting again. For the last month, Henrik had been tracking the shipments of a Bastian-based rye merchant who'd recently started running an unsanctioned side trade in gems. My uncle had paid one of the apprentices in the warehouse to report on his inventory, and three times a week, I was tasked with watching the comings and goings of the shop in the night hours. Every time I saw the gleam in my uncle's eye when I turned in my report, it filled me with dread. Because I knew what that look meant. There was another job coming, and after my failure at the docks, I had a feeling it would fall to me.

A knock at the door downstairs almost broke the rhythm of my counting, but I got to the end of the line, making the note on the parchment. And then another.

"Who's asking?" Murrow's voice drifted up from the street to the open window, finding me.

I finished the sums, checking my watch again. One hour and fifty minutes. I sighed, snapping the ledger shut and getting to my feet. The door of my room screeched as I opened it and came down the steps, straightening my shirt and checking that it was tucked in. Henrik didn't like sloppiness, and I needed to be on his good side if I was going to slip his notice come sundown.

"And who the *hell* are you?" Henrik's voice echoed, traveling up the stairwell from below.

I bristled. All I needed was for him to be in a bad mood when I gave him the ledger. No one knocked on that door without an invitation. If there was one thing Henrik hated, it was outsiders.

"Who the hell are *you*?" another voice snapped.

I stopped midstride when I heard it, one hand gripping the railing so tight that I thought my knuckles would crack. That deep, even voice.

"*Shit.*" I raced down the steps, coming around the corner, and froze when I saw them.

Murrow and Henrik stood against the wall of the sitting room in their bright white shirts, staring at Paj like they were ready to cut out his tongue. The handle of my uncle's knife stuck out of the belt at his back, and any moment, it would be in his hand. When that happened, all my uncles would be coming through the workshop door.

Paj stood taller than both of them, a scowl on his face.

They turned their attention to me and the weight of the house seemed to suddenly be pressing down upon me, making me feel like I was going to fall over.

"Auster." Paj said my name.

But it wasn't the placid tone of business. There was a familiarity in his voice. I watched as my uncle's face was instantly set aflame. Beside him, Murrow's indignant composure broke. He looked rattled. I could see him pivoting in his mind, trying to decide what to do next.

"Well?" Henrik roared. "Who exactly is this?"

"A trader," I stammered, looking between them. "I've—

39

I've been working him at the docks." My voice sounded hollow. Panicked. That wasn't good.

Paj grimaced, his lips parting, but anything he said next would be the wrong thing. Before he could speak, I stepped forward, pushing the ledger into my uncle's chest. "I'm sorry. He's not supposed to be here."

Henrik spoke slowly. "Get. Him. Out of here." The words boiled with rage.

I drew in a breath, willing my heartbeat to slow before I turned to face Paj. He was still staring at me, a fire lit in his eyes. "Come on." I stepped past him, pulling the door open. I waited for him to go out before I followed.

I heard the door lock behind me and I took off, walking with measured steps up the street. But I was breathing so hard that my head felt as if it were stuffed with cotton. Already, my mind was whirling with every possibility. Every scenario in which Henrik put together what I'd been up to. Each one had an ending I didn't like.

I didn't stop until I reached an alley on the other side of Lower Vale. I turned into it, checking the windows overhead before I turned on Paj. "What was that?"

"What?" He gaped at me. "I could ask you the same thing."

"What are you doing here?"

A strange sound escaped his throat. "We docked early. I came to find you," he said, bewildered.

"You can't just come here!" I rasped, taking a fistful of his shirt.

Paj shoved me off. "I didn't know."

"I thought it was implied." I cursed under my breath. "You know who I am." I ran my hands over my face, breathing through my fingers. "What the hell were you thinking?"

He was stoic, his eyes growing colder by the second. "I didn't mean to get you in trouble."

"You—" I scoffed. "You think *that's* what I'm worried about? I don't want you anywhere near my family."

Paj looked so confused that I almost felt sorry for him. He had no idea. No idea what he'd risked just by knocking on that door. And I was suddenly so aware of how thoughtless it had been of me to go to the docks and wait for him two weeks ago. What the hell was *I* thinking?

"Just . . . ," I said, calmer, "you just can't come here again. Ever."

He pressed his lips together and I was suddenly grateful I couldn't hear whatever he was thinking. "Don't worry. I won't," he said flatly. He moved around me, stepping back out into the street, and disappeared into the stream of people flooding out of Lower Vale.

I leaned into the wall and lowered myself to my haunches, waiting for my breathing to calm. If I walked back into the house like this, my uncle would be all over me. I knew Henrik, and that was the problem. Because he also knew me. I'd spent my entire life being a perfect son of Roth. I obeyed the rules. I did what I was told. I didn't question or argue. It was the reason I'd stayed in my uncle's good graces.

When I finally did come back through the door, Henrik's

office was open. I stopped before it, closing my eyes and praying to whatever gods existed before I went inside.

He sat at the desk, copying the ledger I'd given him. "What have I told you about outsiders?" he muttered.

"It won't happen again," I answered.

It was the first rule of this house. The second was no lies. I could see the wheels in my uncle's head turning slowly. Methodically. There was nothing more terrifying.

"Better not." He lifted his eyes. They glimmered with the firelight that danced in the room.

When he said nothing else, I left and let the door close behind me.

I went back up the stairs, and I could feel him in the room before I even came through my bedroom door. Murrow sat in the chair tucked into the corner, one foot propped up on the other knee. His hands were folded in his lap as he looked at me, waiting.

I closed the door and leaned into the wall, staring at the floor.

"Is there something you want to tell me?" he said, keeping his voice low.

I swallowed. "No."

"You sure about that? Because I can't look out for you if I don't know what's going on."

I finally met his eyes. Murrow and Ezra were the only two people in the world I had ever trusted. If I'd told him about Paj, he would have been able to fix the situation at the door before Henrik ever knew he was there. The only protection either of us had from our uncle's wrath was each other.

I sighed. "It's that trader. The one from the *Scourge*."

Both of his eyebrows lifted. "You have got to be kidding me." A smile broke on his lips.

I winced. "I know."

Murrow sighed, getting back to his feet. "You are seriously screwed."

"Yeah." I could feel the burn in my cheeks.

"Might want to let him know that next time he knocks on the door he could lose a hand. Or two," he quipped, "Need me to cover for you for a few hours?"

I snatched my jacket from the chair. "Thanks."

"Aus," he said. I stopped, looking back at him. But the rueful smile was missing from his lips now. "Be careful."

FIVE

I walked the streets of North End as the sun went down, but if Paj had been there, he was already gone.

I didn't want to risk asking for him at the docks. There were too many people who knew my face and no good would come to a trader who had a Roth keeping tabs on them. Instead, I went to the tavern and took my usual seat, hoping that sometime in the night, he might show.

The barkeep set down a bottle of rye and a single glass, but I couldn't bring myself to drink it. I turned around on the stool so that I could see the doors to the street as they opened and closed. The tavern was mostly filled with the same faces, and tonight, no one from my family was on duty.

The sound of rain rumbled outside as darkness fell over the city one painstaking minute at a time. I checked my watch over and over. If Paj had gone back to the ship for the night, he wouldn't likely leave again before they set sail. I'd have to wait until the next time they docked to see him, and that thought made my jaw clench tight.

Nothing was easy in my family. I'd always known that. But I'd never had anything of my own before. My entire world was built upon the framework of my bloodline, and I'd never known anything different. I'd also never had anything to hide from them. But when I'd come down the stairs and seen Paj standing there, for the first time, I did. And that was a perilous place to be.

The worst part was that I'd put myself there. And even though I knew that, I was doing it again by sitting in the tavern, watching the doors and hoping Paj would walk through them.

They opened and closed again and again, and each time, it sent my heart into my throat. But Paj didn't show.

Not until I was sure he wouldn't.

He came in with a group of traders. The hood of his grey jacket glistened with raindrops as he let it fall back. He followed them to a booth in the back corner, but he stopped short when he spotted me at the bar. He hesitated, rubbing a hand over his shaved head before he finally made his way toward me. The heart in my throat suddenly felt as if it had grown spines.

He came to stand at the bar, shaking the rain from his jacket. "Well?" he said with his usual candor. But this time, it was gruff.

I kept my back to the barkeep. "Can we talk?"

"About what?"

I exhaled. He wasn't going to make this easy on me. I didn't blame him. "I'm sorry about before. I—"

"What do you want?" He cut me off.

"To apologize, I guess."

"No, Auster." He didn't look away when he asked it. "What

do you *want*?" His eyes stared into mine, waiting with the same patience that he always seemed to have. Even that night on the docks when he'd had a knife to my throat, he'd looked at me that way.

The barkeep dragged a rag down the counter behind us and I didn't miss the way he glanced up from the corner of his eye. I couldn't afford to have anyone talking. Not after what happened at the house.

I jerked my chin toward the stairs that led up to the tavern's rooms, and Paj exhaled heavily before he nodded. A few minutes after he disappeared up the corridor, I followed, trying the handles of the doors until I found one that was unlocked. When I opened it, Paj was leaning against the opposite wall with his arms crossed over his chest.

It was one of the simple sleeping rooms the tavern rented out, with a single window looking out at a nearly full moon hovering over the rooftops. Beside it, an empty washbowl and pitcher sat on a stand, and a bed dressed with fresh linen was pushed against the wall.

Paj seemed to take up half the room with his silence. He was still waiting for an answer and I didn't know how to get out the only one that I had.

I stood on the other side of the window, trying to summon up the courage to speak. "I'm sorry about what happened at the house. I didn't think you'd come there. If I did, I would have warned you."

"I wanted to see you," he said, not even a hint of reservation behind the words.

How did he do that? Just cut through things and say what he meant?

He waited.

"I don't know how to do this."

"Do what?"

"This." I gestured between us. "My family—"

"I don't care about your stupid family," Paj shot back.

"Well, they *will* care about you. My uncle likes to . . . control things." I paused. That was putting it lightly. "I just can't have them involved. At all."

He considered that for a moment, his mouth twisting to one side. "All right."

The tight coil in my chest unraveled just a little. "All right?"

He nodded, but I could tell he didn't like it. "I won't go back there."

"Thank you."

"But," he added, "I want to know what you do."

"What do you mean?"

"For your family." He sat on the window ledge.

I studied him, looking for some clue of what he was getting at. "I can't really tell you that."

"You don't have to tell me details." He spoke evenly. "But I need to know what kind of person you are."

His meaning came together in the way he looked at me then, and it soured in my stomach. "You want to know if I hurt people."

He nodded.

I fidgeted with the chain of my watch, casting my eyes to the floor. "I don't hurt people. That's not really . . . my job." That was true. We all had roles to fulfill, but that had never been mine. Ezra and my uncle Casimir, on the other hand, had plenty of blood on their hands. "But I'm not going to lie to you. I'm far from innocent."

"I think I pretty much had that figured when I caught you trying to steal from the *Scourge*," he said, almost to himself.

"But you didn't turn me in."

"No, I didn't."

I wanted to ask him why, but there was a part of me that was afraid of the answer. My eyes focused on the air surrounding him. Paj had a calmness I had never seen in anyone, and when he looked at me, he looked deep. Like he could see everything. I had never felt the way I did in that moment as I watched him from across the room, like I was waiting for a storm to swallow me whole.

"I don't like him," he said suddenly.

"Who?"

"Your uncle."

I smirked. "That's a commonly held opinion."

"You still haven't answered my question," he said, and the words he'd spoken downstairs resurfaced.

What do you want, Auster?

I'd hoped he wouldn't make me answer it. I ran a hand through my hair, swallowing. "I wanted to see you too." I sighed. "The only thing I've thought about for the last two weeks is seeing you."

He smiled, changing the way the light hit his eyes. It almost hurt to look at.

I let several seconds pass before I convinced myself to ask. "Do you have to leave?" It came out more revealing than I intended. It sounded like I was asking him not to. And I was.

He thought about his answer before he gave it. "Not until morning."

The part of me that was still holding its breath finally let go. Before I'd even decided to, I was crossing the room, slipping through the beams of moonlight until I was standing in front of him. He didn't move, and I realized he was waiting to see what I would do. He breathed evenly, watching as my hands lifted between us, and I touched his face the way I had imagined, running my thumb along the line of his jaw.

He leaned into my touch, and when his lips parted, I closed the space between us and kissed him slowly, feeling the way our mouths fit together.

His fingers dragged over my arms as he stood, leaving a trail of blazing fire behind, and when he kissed me back, it wasn't gentle. It wasn't patient or calm.

"I didn't either," he whispered between breaths.

"What?"

"Think of anything else."

SIX

I never told him that I didn't sleep those nights.

The flame on the bedside candle traveled down the wick slowly until it drowned in the pool of clear wax below. I'd been watching it for hours, listening to the sound of Paj breathing. He was always so warm, no matter how cold the night. As if the sun that drenched the sea was trapped inside of him. I rarely closed my eyes on nights that he was in Bastian because I was terrified of waking to the sunrise, when he had to go.

It had been almost six months since I'd tried to steal the rye off his ship, and there wasn't a day that passed that I wasn't grateful my uncle had sent me to the docks that night.

Every two weeks, I took a room at the tavern and waited by the window, watching the hands of my watch tick slowly until I heard his footsteps coming up the stairs. Twelve hours later, he was slipping from my arms and back out the door before the harbor bell rang, and that moment was getting harder every time I met it.

He shifted beside me, but his eyes didn't open as his hands

searched beneath the quilt. When they found me, he wrapped an arm around my middle and pressed his face to my back, groaning. He always did that before he got up, as if checking to see if I was still there.

I laced my fingers into his and kissed his knuckles. His hands were calloused and rough from his work on the ship, his skin covered in salt, and there was nothing more beautiful in the world to me.

He let out a heavy breath before he swung his legs to the floor and pulled away from me. The quilt slipped down past his waist and I studied the line of him. He was shaped as if carved from marble, and I had every line of him memorized.

I sat up behind him, running one hand through my mussed hair and smoothing it back. "Do you see anyone at your other ports?" I asked, watching him slip the shirt over his head.

He gave me his lopsided smile. The one he had when he thought I was joking. But it fell when I didn't smile back. "Are you serious?"

"Yeah." It was a question I had wanted to ask him many times but hadn't had the guts to.

Paj stopped fastening the buttons at his wrist, looking suddenly agitated. "Are you trying to tell me something?"

"I'm trying to *ask* you something," I said, confused.

He turned around and the muscles in his back contracted as he buckled his belt. "Do you see anyone when I'm gone?"

I wasn't sure if I'd ever heard that sound in his voice before. He was missing his usual steadiness. In fact, he almost sounded . . . angry.

51

"No."

His jaw clenched. "Would you tell me if you did?"

My eyes narrowed at him. "I was asking if *you* see anyone else."

"Of course I don't. What kind of question is that?"

"We just never talked about it before and I—"

"I don't want to see anyone else," he said sharply. "And I don't want you to see anyone else."

I grinned. He *was* angry.

"What?"

"Nothing." I stifled a laugh.

When he realized I was making fun of him, the crook in his brow softened and he shoved me in the arm. I caught hold of his hand and pulled him toward me. "I don't want to see anyone else either," I said seriously.

His eyes shifted back and forth on mine before he nodded. I knew him well enough now to recognize when he was relieved. He touched his forehead to mine before he kissed me on the cheek and stood back up, then sat in the chair in the corner so he could pull on his boots one at a time.

The truth was I didn't even think about anyone else. The thought of not being with Paj was like a hole in my chest that only closed when he was there. I spent almost as much time being afraid of what that meant as I did thinking about him. Because I'd known months ago there would come a time when I couldn't be without him anymore. But I wasn't ready to tell him that yet.

A knock sounded at the door and we both stilled, our eyes

meeting before he went to stand against the wall. I slid out of the bed, pulling on my trousers. When I reached the door, I opened it just enough to see Greta, the kitchen maid.

"Morning." She held a small tray set with tea, cheese, and bread in her hands.

"Thank you." I took it, closing the door with my foot, and Paj locked it behind me as I set the tray on the little table beside the window.

He poured the tea as I dropped the sugar cubes into both cups and then dribbled a few splashes of milk into his. We had a rhythm that was familiar now, down to the way his hand absently opened for mine when he stretched it between us.

"What are you doing over the next two weeks?" He didn't glance up when he said it, but I could hear the real question in his voice. The one he wasn't supposed to ask.

"Come on, Paj," I said, trying to keep my tone light.

"I just want to know what you do when I'm gone." He tried to play it off, but he wasn't any good at pretending. That was one of the things I loved about him.

I set down the spoon. "We agreed we wouldn't talk about my family."

He placed his elbows onto the table and laced his fingers together, staring at them. "I worry about you, that's all."

That was why we didn't talk about it. Because he and I both knew he had reason to worry. I was doing dangerous work. I'd been doing dangerous work for my uncle since I was a child.

"Every time you leave, it feels like longer than the last time," I said, changing the subject.

He gave me a smile, looking more like himself, and I relaxed a little. I didn't like it when he left with things unsaid, but there would always be things unsaid between us. That was something I tried not to think about.

Another knock sounded at the door and I got back to my feet. This time, Murrow stood in the hallway, and I immediately bristled, eyeing the stairs behind him that led down to the tavern.

"I'm alone." He answered my unspoken question, gesturing for me to let him in.

I stepped back to open the door and he ducked inside.

"Hey, Paj."

"Hey." Paj stood, giving Murrow his hand.

It was much to my relief that the two of them liked each other, but Murrow had made no secret of the fact that he thought I was playing with fire. I hadn't once argued with him. He was right.

There were rules in our family about everything, including love. Bringing someone in wasn't a simple decision, and it required the approval of not only Henrik but all of my uncles. But even if being honest with my family about Paj would make things easier, there were many ways in which it would make things harder.

Murrow glanced between Paj and me awkwardly, and I let out a frustrated breath. Whatever he'd come to talk about, it was family business.

"It's all right, I have to go anyway." Paj took his jacket from where it was draped over the chair before he kissed me, once on the lips and once on the cheek. "I'll see you."

"I'll see you," I said, watching him slip out the door.

When I turned back to the window, Murrow was already devouring the bread and cheese. "Couldn't wait an hour?" I sank back into the chair, glaring at him.

"Not really."

"Then it better be important."

Murrow spoke with a full mouth, taking a sip of Paj's tea before he'd even swallowed. "Isn't it always?"

"Okay, so, what is it?"

Murrow's gaze moved around the room and the hair on my arms instantly stood on end. "Henrik heard that rye merchant has a cache of emeralds leaving tomorrow. He wants the switch done today."

"Today?" I snapped. "We aren't supposed to do it for another month. We're not ready."

Murrow shrugged and took another bite.

I shook my head, cursing. "We're not ready," I said again.

Murrow's eyebrows lifted knowingly. "Try telling Henrik that."

I shoved the plate away from me, leaning back into the chair. The light from the window warmed the glass, melting the thin bit of frost that was etched there, and I tried to make out the harbor below. Only a few masts were poking out of the fog. In another hour, Paj would be disappearing over the horizon.

"It'll be fine," he said. "It's always fine, right?"

I shook my head, pinching my eyes closed so that I could go through it in my mind. The apprentice Henrik paid off only worked in the shop at night, so we wouldn't have his help. I'd seen enough buyers come in and strike deals to know how it would play out, but I didn't like it when plans changed. That was how my aunt Eden and uncle Tomlin had gotten a knife in their backs on a job gone wrong.

"We'll need Ezra," I said finally.

Murrow nodded. "I figured. Told him to be ready after breakfast."

I stared at the table, trying to think. There were more than a few things that could go wrong and this time, it wasn't just Sowan rye at stake. These were emeralds, and the gem guild wouldn't look the other way if we were caught.

"Barkeep said you were up here with *the trader* when I came in," Murrow said, draining the cup of tea. "You need to be more careful. People talk."

"I'm tired of being careful," I said, my voice thin.

I could see by the look in Murrow's eyes that he knew what I meant. We'd spent our entire lives being careful. To the world we were Roths, marked with a name that would never leave us. But even beneath our uncle's roof, we weren't free from harm. Here, between the walls of this little room, was the only place I felt safe.

"Just watch out, yeah?" he said more gently.

I nodded, taking a deep breath before I stood and pulled my shirt on. I buttoned it methodically and tucked it in before I shrugged on the vest and fastened it. Then I combed my hair back and brushed off my trousers, checking my shoes for scuffs before I slipped them on. When I finally let my eyes lift to the mirror, a reflection I knew well looked back. A smartly dressed Roth in a clean white shirt and a suit fit for the Merchant's District. But I wasn't sure who I was beneath it anymore.

SEVEN

Azimuth House stood at the mouth of the Merchant's District. It was the home of Holland, the most successful gem merchant in Bastian, and beyond it stretched a tangle of the most prestigious shops and estates.

Henrik knew better than to step foot in this district because there weren't many merchants in Bastian who didn't want him dead. There wasn't a single one of them who hadn't been touched by his schemes with gem fakes, but somehow, he always came out of the other side with his head.

That wasn't the only reason they hated him. I had never seen anyone as good with the stones as Henrik was, and he had something that no one else did—Ezra. Henrik had snatched up the exceptionally talented silversmith from the coal fire of a small shop when he was a soot-covered ten-year-old.

My grandfather Felix had built our trade in the shadows on fake gems, but it was a merchant's ring Henrik was after. One day, he said, he'd have a shop in the Merchant's District. But no one in their right mind was going to give him a merchant's ring when everyone in Bastian had been on the receiving end of his work.

"There," Ezra whispered, tapping my elbow with his.

Across the cobblestone street, a man walked behind a wheeled cart being pulled by two men. It creaked along, the joints struggling even though there was only one thing loaded—a chest. If the cart was that heavy, there could only be one thing in the trunk—coin. And lots of it.

Murrow clicked his tongue beside me. "He's practically asking to be robbed."

But we weren't after the coin. Not this time.

The man likely worked for one of the big trading ships down in the harbor and the only reason he would be hauling that much coin into a shop in this district was for a pickup of gemstones. But he wasn't headed to a gem merchant. He was stopping at the door of a rye merchant.

It wasn't unusual for merchants from other guilds to have a side trade of gemstones. But this merchant's side trade had been moving a cache of rare emeralds. How they were getting to other ports was the tricky part. It had taken me months to figure out that he was stowing them in crates of expensive rye.

These particular stones weren't supposed to be picked up for another month, and by a different buyer. If the plans had changed, the apprentice had either lied to us or a higher bidder came into play. I guessed it was the latter. If I was wrong, we were screwed.

"I don't feel good about this," I muttered, watching the man.

"Like we have a choice." Murrow scoffed.

Behind him, Ezra looked as skeptical as I was. Making this switch in the middle of the day with no plan was going to get all three of us killed. But Henrik had been working on these emeralds for weeks and the payoff was more than the Roths had seen in a single job for years.

These weren't just any gems, either. They were cat's-eye emeralds, named for the gleam of light that banded down the center, making it look like a pupil. Henrik had been working on the fakes for months until he perfected the technique, and now an entire purse full of the fakes was heavy in my vest pocket. Henrik had given me his nicest jacket so that I wouldn't look out of place in the shop, but it didn't matter how much I blended in. If I didn't do this right, the merchant would know in seconds what I was up to.

The man on the street had the chest unloaded and three of them disappeared inside the shop, leaving the empty cart behind. It would take another five minutes or so for the merchant to retrieve the stones for the buyer and once they were in view, I could make the switch.

"So? What's the plan?" Murrow asked. It was my job to switch the stones, but it was Murrow and Ezra's job to distract the merchant and cover my tracks.

But the plan had gone out the window. "You'll think of something." I took off across the street, not looking back.

I opened the door of the shop just as the two men who'd unloaded the chest came out. They struck up their pipes and perched themselves against the window and I stepped inside, keeping my face turned toward the counter. If I gave them my back, they'd watch me, and I couldn't afford to draw their attention.

The merchant stood behind the wooden counter, a wall of shelves reaching to the ceiling behind him. They were stocked with everything from poor man's rye to the expensive bottles from Nimsmire and the Sowan-stamped labels of the Narrows.

"Be with you in a moment," the merchant mumbled, not looking up.

The buyer stood at the counter with both hands set on the glass, a pair of spectacles pulled up to sit on top of his head. In the corner, an apprentice was prying open a new crate that had just arrived. This wasn't the apprentice Henrik had in his pocket. This was a girl I'd seen many times as I watched the place. She was quiet and solemn and my gut told me she couldn't be bought.

The buyer watched her with an air of boredom, his bottom lip sticking out and his chin puckered, as the merchant discretely lined up the stones for inspection on a swatch of black silk. No one in the Merchant's District was going to report their most beloved rye merchant for moving a few stones. But little did the guilds know, this man's business rivaled some of the gem merchants whose shops neighbored his.

I walked along the wall of bottles slowly, feigning interest in the handwritten labels. But I was listening, trying to determine how many people were working in the back room. Only one set of footsteps sounded on the brick floor, followed by a few echoes.

"Anything I can help with?" the merchant inquired, losing his patience with my lurking presence.

I smiled. "Have a question about a shipment coming in. I'll wait."

"All right."

Sunlight gleamed on the emeralds as the merchant shifted the tray into the light and the buyer picked up different ones for inspection. But I was counting. The number had to be right, and if the apprentice who'd been working with Henrik had missed even one stone, this wasn't going to work.

Twenty-eight. That's what it looked like, and that was the right number. But I couldn't see over the closest lip of the tray to be absolutely sure. It would have to do.

Just as I thought it, the sound of voices made the merchant look up over his spectacles. Outside the window, Murrow and Ezra were talking to the two men who'd pulled the cart up from the harbor.

"Everything look good?" The merchant turned his attention back to the stones and the buyer nodded. "Weigh them and I'll be on my way."

The merchant nodded and shuffled to the back wall, where three sets of scales were set up. He stepped to one side so that the buyer could watch him load the largest scale and see the readings clearly. When he was satisfied, the merchant brought them back and set the tray down.

I tried to will my heartbeat to slow as he piled them into a bag and tied it closed. While their eyes were focused on the dial, I reached into my jacket and pulled the purse of fakes free. The color was a perfect replica, the edges of the stones etched by hand to mimic the cut of a dredger's chisel. Even the weight was correct, a skill that Henrik guarded with the utmost secrecy and hadn't passed on to a single member of the family. Not yet, anyway.

The voices outside grew louder and the merchant looked up again, shaking his head with a sigh. Murrow and Ezra were now arguing with the two men at the cart. The buyer watched them with his face twisted up like a screw. But when Murrow shoved one of them back and the man stumbled into the window, the merchant stopped what he was doing.

"What the—" He came around the corner, throwing the door open with the buyer on his heels.

"Get out of here!" the buyer bellowed, cursing at Murrow, who was still shouting.

I took the chance because it was the only one I was going to get. I put myself between the apprentice and the tray, still watching the street as I deftly set down the bag of fakes. The merchant was already waddling back inside and when the bell on the door jingled, the apprentice looked up from the open crate at her feet.

Shit.

I slid my elbow across the surface of the glass, knocking a stack of bottles from where they stood at the end of the counter. They crashed to the floor, shattering into pieces. The apprentice gasped, lunging forward and sinking to the floor. As soon as she disappeared, I swiped the emeralds and tucked them into my vest.

"Hey." The apprentice's voice was the only thing I could hear over my pounding heart.

My eyes slid to the side, finding her. She was crouched on the other side of the counter, her eyes on my jacket.

"Did you just . . ." She sprang to her feet. "Hey!"

I threw myself toward the door, but the buyer had me by the collar in the next breath, jerking me backward. I turned, slipping from the jacket, and the seams popped as I tore free. But as I pivoted, a sudden, sharp blow caught me below the ribs. When I looked down, the buyer's hand was clutched around the handle of a small knife, its blade buried in my side.

My breaths slowed as I stared down at it, red blooming on my white shirt.

The girl behind the counter screamed and Ezra barreled through the door. He had his blade out in the next second, and when the man turned on him, Ezra caught him by the throat with one hand and drove his knife into the buyer's gut.

A gargled sound escaped his mouth and Ezra dropped him on the floor, his furious gaze tightening when his eyes trailed down to my blood-soaked shirt. He yanked me forward, throwing my arm over his shoulder. "You're all right." His deep voice reverberated inside my head, making me dizzy.

Somehow, we were already outside. Walking across the street. But the sun was too bright. The street too loud.

I clutched at his jacket when I couldn't draw a chest full of air and he squeezed my wrist. "Breathe. I've got you. Keep walking."

Murrow was waiting for us around the corner of the next

64

alley, and when he saw the handle of the knife, his eyes went wide. "Shit. Shit, shit, shit."

"Give him your jacket," Ezra ordered, setting me against the wall.

Murrow obeyed, tearing it off and then sliding it up my arms. As soon as the knife was concealed, we were walking again, Murrow in front and Ezra at my side.

I don't remember the walk to Lower Vale. I don't know if I even stayed on my own two feet. The next thing I remember is lying on the table in my uncle's house with my clothes cut off and Henrik cursing at the physician. The smear of my blood on my uncle's hands. The way his hair uncharacteristically fell into his face, making him look like a stranger. I could see his lips moving, but I couldn't hear the words.

I let my head lean back, watching the baubles on the chandelier hanging from the ceiling and remembering the little flame on the candle that morning as Paj slept. The way it shrank as it slid down the wick. And the little ribbon of smoke when, at last, it flickered out.

EIGHT

For the first time, I was dreading Paj's return.

I stood in front of the mirror with my shirt open, pressing around the edges of the wound in my side. The planes of my stomach curved down and around to the perfectly straight slash, where the skin was still puckered with stitched black thread. It had taken days for the blood to stop seeping, ruining more than a few crisp white shirts that Sylvie would never get clean, but for once, my uncle hadn't balked.

"Looks good." Henrik admired the carve of red below my ribs. He seemed to be genuinely proud.

I could barely recall the hours of the physician working to close up the gash, but I did clearly remember giving my uncle those emeralds. I hadn't even thought twice when I reached into my vest and handed them over. I was bleeding, the edges of black pushing in around my mind, and still, all I could think of was to give him those damn gems.

Lucky, the physician had said. Lucky the buyer at the shop was lousy with a knife, that is. But that didn't matter now. The poor bastard was dead.

"Haven't heard a peep from the rye guild. We won't unless that merchant wants them to find out about his little gem trade."

The buyer's death was chalked up to an unfortunate misunderstanding, and Henrik had gotten everything he wanted. As usual.

I was just glad to have my life.

The emeralds were already sorted into trays down in Henrik's workshop because the fakes were *that* good. Only a gem sage would be able to spot them and those were rare these days.

Henrik laughed, clapping me on the back, and I winced, sucking in a breath. The pain was still deep and raw, even two weeks later, and the stitches pulled every time I moved.

Ezra caught my eyes in the mirror as Henrik left the room, but he was unreadable, as always. His silver-scarred arms were crossed in front of him over his leather apron. He hadn't flinched when he stabbed the gem buyer, and I couldn't see any trace of guilt on his face about it now. Behind him, Murrow was watching me with a worried expression. He hadn't said much about that day, and even now, he deliberately didn't look at the wound in my side. If I didn't know better, I'd think it had scared him.

"Cover for me?" I said, pulling up my suspenders.

"Sure." Ezra was the one to answer.

They'd been covering for me for months now. I'd run out of reasons for disappearing a long time ago and it had been Murrow and Ezra who'd crafted the lies for me. Usually, I didn't care what they were. I just wanted to see Paj. But today, I had lingered longer than usual and I knew I was avoiding the tavern.

Ezra left without another word, but Murrow stayed, one hip leaning into the windowsill.

"I'm sorry," he said.

I straightened my vest. "Sorry for what?"

"You told me we shouldn't do it and I just went along with what Henrik said anyway."

"It wouldn't have mattered." I scoffed. Henrik wouldn't have budged. But when I looked up, Murrow wasn't laughing, like he usually did. He looked sick.

"I—" He paled. "I thought you were going to die."

I took the opportunity to turn back to the mirror when a lump rose in my throat. The truth was, I thought I was going to die too. And I wouldn't be the first Roth to give their life for the family business.

"Well, I didn't die," I said finally.

"No, you didn't." He said, looking a bit more like himself.

He went down the stairs and I tucked my watch into my vest, listening for Henrik to make his way into the workshop before I slipped out of the house.

I walked the streets of Lower Vale until I saw the tavern at the top of the hill. The evenings were warmer and each day was growing longer as the seasons changed. But this sunset was particularly brilliant, painting the sky with bold amber strokes. There was a small twist in my stomach as I reached the doors and I breathed through it, stepping inside. The barkeep watched me from behind the counter, but I ignored him, my eyes on the dark stairs. I could see the candlelight beneath the door by the time I reached the top, and I steeled myself. Paj was already waiting.

I put on my best charming smile and knocked. Paj's footsteps crossed the floor, growing louder, and the door opened. Water dripped from his face in glistening rivers and the cloth that was usually draped over the washbowl was crumpled in his hands.

He smiled widely, not even waiting for me to get out of the hallway before he kissed me. His skin was warm and his mouth tasted of salt, like it always did when he got in. The twist in my belly uncurled, traveling up to my chest until I could hardly swallow. Tears stung the corners of my eyes and I blinked furiously before they could fall.

I hadn't let myself think about it, warding away the faintest shadow of the possibility. That I would have never seen him again if . . .

He closed the door behind me and wiped the water from his face, dragging the cloth beneath his chin. "Swiped some cava from the cargo hull." He smirked, gesturing to a tall skinny bottle on the little table.

I picked it up, turning it in my hands. The wax-sealed cork was stamped with the Nimsmire port seal and inside, the clear liquid bubbled. But I was still trying to breathe through the pain in my chest.

"You all right?" His look turned just the slightest bit watchful.

"Yeah." I smiled, setting it back down. "I missed you."

He tossed the cloth toward the washbowl and took the two steps between us. I held my breath as his hands lifted and gently brushed the hair back out of my face. "I missed you," he said in his even, steady tone. He always talked like that, as if he simply meant exactly what he said. There was never anything hiding beneath his words.

I held onto his shirt and pulled him toward me until my lips were pressed to his and his arms came around me. The tenderness in my side instantly woke, but I didn't care. I wanted him to hold me so tightly. And he did. He folded himself around me, tucking his face into the corner of my shoulder and my neck. I let out a tight breath when the throb under my ribs sent a wave of agony through me.

His grip on me instantly loosened and he pulled away, eyes traveling over my face. "What's wrong?"

"Nothing." My voice was still tight.

He looked serious now. "What's wrong, Auster?"

I forced another smile, but it was weak. "I have these stupid stitches in my side. They sting every time I move."

"Stitches? For what?" He was already opening my jacket and pushing it down my arms.

But this was the moment I'd been dreading. The one I'd known I couldn't avoid.

He tugged the tail of my shirt from where it was tucked into my trousers and lifted until he saw it. He stiffened, going so still that I couldn't tell if he was breathing.

"It's just few stitches." I laughed, but there was a sheen of sweat across my brow.

Paj was still staring at it, the pulse at his neck jumping. "What happened?"

This was it—a defining moment. I had never lied to him about anything. Ever. And I still hadn't decided if this was the moment I'd finally do it.

His eyes raised slowly to meet mine, then narrowed, as if he could hear my thoughts. "If you think I don't know what a knife wound looks like, you're an idiot. Tell me what happened."

I was almost relieved that he'd made the decision for me. But whatever was coming next wasn't going to be pleasant. "A job," I said simply.

"A job," he repeated.

"It didn't go as planned." I pushed my shirt back down. "It happens."

Paj stared at me wordlessly, his breaths deep and controlled.

"It's how I met you, if you remember."

A look of disbelief surfaced on his face. "That's not funny. *This* isn't funny."

I bit the inside of my cheek, embarrassed. "I know it's not. I'm sorry."

There was a war behind Paj's eyes. A glimmer of fury that looked like it would ignite at any moment. "When are we going talk about this?"

I felt small in the room, the pain in my side making me lightheaded. "We agreed—"

"I don't care what we agreed." He leveled his eyes at me, his jaw clenching.

I had feared a moment like this for months. Because I was

in this. All the way. And that meant there would come a time when Paj had to make peace with my family and who we were. If he didn't, one of us would have to walk away, and I already knew it wasn't going to be me.

"This is exactly what I was afraid of happening," he rasped. "And who the hell did he call when you were bleeding to death? I could have stitched it better myself." He flung a hand at me.

I'd been prepared for this. "What you do is dangerous and what I do is dangerous. That's just how it is." I recited the practiced words. "I worry about you. I worry every time there's a storm. Or if the ship comes in late, I worry."

He shook his head. "That's different."

"No, it's not."

"Auster." He was on the edge of shouting. "When are you going to admit that this is not okay?"

"It doesn't matter if it's okay. This is my life." My voice rose. "This is what my life is."

"No. Your family—"

"I don't want to talk about my family!" I snapped.

Paj stared at me blankly. "Why not? We talk about everything else."

The truth was a twisted one. It wasn't just that the Roths had rules or that I didn't want to argue with Paj. Part of it was and would always be that I still felt like I needed to defend them. Even though I knew how illogical that was.

"Because I just want to . . ." I exhaled, frustrated. "I want to pretend like my family doesn't exist."

At that, his face softened, and a heavy breath escaped his lips. I didn't realize I was crying until he reached up and wiped a tear from my cheek, and I took hold of his arm, pressing his hand against me so that I could feel his warmth.

"Why can't you understand that?" I whispered.

He searched my eyes and when he said the words, they spun in the air between us. "Because I love you." He spoke quietly. Tenderly. "*I want to be your family.*"

The sound broke something open inside of me. Something painful and at the same time, healing. I let it spill into the corners of my heart until I felt as if I was going to melt into him. I wanted to take the words and write them over my body the way the mark of the Roths stained my skin. I wanted to tell a new story with them. But I didn't know how.

This wasn't like what I'd seen with Ezra or Murrow or any of my uncles. It wasn't a fleeting infatuation intensified by secret nights in the tavern. This was like the rarest throw of dice in Three Widows—triple stars.

I loved him too. I knew that. This thing I felt had a hold on me. It was becoming more deeply rooted by the day. But if I said it now, it would destroy me. There weren't many things that were true in the world I lived in, but there was one thing that would never change, no matter who I loved.

I would always be a Roth.

NINE

There were two kinds of days after that—days when I was whole, and days when I wasn't.

The days I was whole were the days when I was with Paj. The others were the days that I missed him.

We didn't talk about what happened again, but it seemed that the tighter the bond cinched between us, the greater the distance too. There had always been things unsaid, but their number was growing. In the weeks after Paj told me he loved me, he'd become more rigid. Less guarded. I caught him staring at the scar below my ribs many times, and when he said goodbye, it was without meeting my eyes. I didn't know if he was pulling away from me or if he was protecting himself from me. Both would break my heart.

I stood at the window in the tavern, watching the stars stretch up over the water as the sky darkened. That night, some feeling nagged at the back of my mind as I waited for him. It crept over my skin, a cold whisper I couldn't ignore. He was late. It didn't happen often, but there were weeks when the *Scourge* didn't arrive to port on time, slowed by weak winds or delayed by a storm.

When another hour passed and Paj still didn't show, I grabbed my jacket from the chair and opened the door. The tavern was bustling below, filled with traders, but when I spotted a couple of faces from Paj's crew, I didn't see him with them.

The street was empty as the rain fell, filling the veins of the cobblestones until they spilled over. My boots splashed in the puddles and I pulled my hood up, taking the fastest route down to the harbor. My breath fogged in front of me as I walked, and with every step, that feeling in my gut tightened.

The stitches in my side had been taken out weeks ago, leaving behind a nasty scar, but the pain was almost gone now. My uncle's grip had loosened on me too, as if the whole ordeal had earned me some kind of twisted trust. I'd used it to take advantage of every minute with Paj I could get, and I'd even begun to consider telling Henrik about him. But each time, I talked myself out of it as quickly as the thought surfaced.

Paj loved me, but I didn't know if he'd sell his soul for me. And if he became one of the Roths, that's exactly what he'd have to do. The even bigger question was how far I was willing to go. Because making Paj a Roth was like cursing him. And that wasn't love.

The harbor was only barely lit in the downpour, but as soon as I started down the hill, I could see it—the *Scourge*. The ship was anchored, its sails rolled up tight, and the deck was dark. As if they'd arrived hours ago.

I waited for the harbor watch to pass the archway before I took the stairs down and picked up my pace, following the main dock until I reached the slip. The ship's cargo was unloaded on the platform ahead and any moment, someone from the Merchant District would be here to pick it up.

As soon as I saw the figure standing at the end of the dock, I let out a relieved breath. Rain soaked his jacket, dripping from the hem as he watched the trail of lights along the shore ahead. He didn't turn around as I came up the dock, weaving in and out of the barrels.

"Paj?" I called out over the sound of the rain.

He looked back over his shoulder, bristling just a little when he saw me. I watched as he glanced up and down the dock warily. For what, I didn't know.

"What are you doing?" As soon as I took a step toward him, he turned, picking up one of the crates nearest to him and moving it to the side clumsily.

"I volunteered for pickup."

"Why?" I said, confused. "I was waiting for you."

He cleared his throat, hauling up another crate and setting it down. "Go home, Auster."

It took me another moment of watching him to realize that he was just re-stacking the crates next to each other. Giving himself something to do so he didn't have to face me. I took another tentative step toward him and reached out, turning him around. Paj's face was hidden in the darkness of his hood. He jerked away from me.

"What's going on?"

He shifted nervously on his feet, his hands finding his pockets. He said it all in one short, rushed breath. "I don't want to do this anymore."

"Do what?"

He shrugged, clearly exasperated. "Me and you."

Those three words were like breaking glass inside my skull. I watched him carefully. I could see the tip of his chin in the moonlight, but he was keeping one shoulder pointed at me, like he didn't want to move further into the light. The cold whisper that had found me at the tavern turned to ice on my skin.

I reached for him but he took a step back, putting more space between us.

"I don't want to see you anymore." He said it slower this time.

The reluctant creep of fear inside of me was igniting into panic. Something was wrong. Very wrong. "Why are you saying that?"

Paj was quiet, as if trying to string together a sequence of words that would make some sense. When I moved toward him again, his back hit the crates behind him, giving him nowhere to go. I reached up, pushing his hood back, and when the light from the streetlamp hit him, I froze.

His face was bloodied and swollen, the bridge of his nose busted beneath his black eyes. He didn't look at me, fixing his stare to the side of the ship.

"What . . . who did this?" I reached up, wiping the blood from his jaw, but again, he shoved me off.

"No one."

My eyes searched his, my pulse climbing. Paj wasn't a stranger to violence. Traders dealt with crew disputes or fights at port all the time. But this was different. He didn't look angry. He looked hurt.

"Tell me who did this and I'll take care of it," I said, my voice sounding strange. I may not have been the one my uncle sent to enact consequences for crossing the family, but I'd pulled my knife more times than I could count. I'd never been hungrier to use it in my life than that moment.

Paj turned away from me again. "No, you won't."

"Paj—"

"Go *home*, Auster," he said weakly.

A thought wove into my mind as I studied the shape of the swelling on his cheek. Somehow, I already knew.

Henrik.

"He was here?" My heart raced. "He came here?"

Paj didn't answer. I could see the collar of his shirt inside the opening of his jacket. The white fabric was spotted with blood where it had dripped from his face.

"He did this to you?" My voice broke. Henrik had been here and he'd put his hands on Paj, but it wasn't as simple as that. There was more to it. "What did he say?" I asked, afraid of the answer.

"That we're done," he answered.

Henrik's relaxed manner over the last month suddenly made sense. He wasn't giving me more trust. He was just getting ready to bring me back in line. "What did he threaten you with?"

Paj raked one hand over his shaved head. "He didn't threaten me." He breathed. "He threatened you."

The tingling on my skin was now a blazing fire.

"So, we're done." He finally met my eyes. There was a finality in them that crushed me.

I could see that he meant it. That was the thing about Paj. He didn't say anything he didn't mean. As his gaze met mine, it was filled with something I feared more than anything else— a goodbye.

"But . . ." I couldn't hear the word I'd spoken.

"Please." His voice wavered. "Just go. And don't come back."

I recoiled, drawing back from him. My hand slipped from his wet jacket and the cold air stung inside my lungs as I drew it into my chest. "I'm not leaving," I spoke through clenched teeth.

"Yes, you are."

"No, I'm not," I said.

He cursed under his breath, pacing to the end of the dock and back. I could see his mind racing. He was scared and the sight of him like that terrified me.

When he finally turned back to me, his face was broken, his eyes pleading. "Watch!"

I stilled, my heart dropping to my gut.

"Watch!" he called out, louder.

"What are you doing?" I whispered hoarsely.

Boots pounded down the docks and two torches appeared in the distance. They drifted toward us.

"Thief!" Paj pinched his eyes closed as he shouted it.

I stared at him, stunned. I couldn't move.

The footsteps grew closer until they were encircling me. Then hands were grabbing at my jacket, dragging me forward. But I was still staring at Paj, my chest hollowed out of every warm thing.

"Caught him trying to make off with the crates of rye." He swallowed. Two tears slipped down his cheeks. And the last words I heard him speak were like a tidal wave, sweeping me beneath it. "I think he's a Roth."

TEN

I stared at the worn, weathered floorboards of the merchant's house as my uncle's voice bled into echoes at the back of my mind. The storm that had been lurking out at sea was now trapped inside me. With every passing second, it was tearing me to pieces, but on the outside, I felt dead. Numb.

There was little that happened on the docks that Henrik didn't know about, and it had taken him less than an hour to show up banging at the door. He was the rottenest of bastards, but my uncle didn't send an errand boy when one of his own was picked up by the watch. He went himself.

"I'm sure you'll agree that there's been some kind of mistake," I heard him say. But I didn't care. Every inch of my skin felt iced over. Not from the freezing rain, but from the howling wind inside of me.

I'd never felt the kind of cold as I did when the watch was hauling me up the dock. Paj didn't look at me. He was facing the black water, and that was the moment when a stillness erupted around me, halting my erratic heartbeat and hitched breath. I stopped fighting the watch, letting them shove me forward, and I didn't hear another sound as the sight of him disappeared around the bow of the *Scourge*.

Words crumbled into dust as they asked my name and what I was doing at the docks. It wasn't until Henrik arrived that I even remembered where I was. But I couldn't find it in me to care.

From the corner of my eye, I saw my uncle pull a purse of coin from his jacket and hand it over. There wasn't a soul in Bastian who couldn't be bought. Not even the harbor watch. Maybe Paj knew that when he did what he did. Maybe he'd known my family would come and fetch me. Take me away. But that didn't matter now because Paj was gone. And the only thing worse than the words he'd said was the fact that he'd meant them.

Something heavy landed on my shoulder, making me flinch, and I blinked, my eyes refocusing. When I looked up, Henrik was standing over me, one thumb hooked into the pocket of his vest. His sleeves were half rolled up, the button at his neck undone. He wasn't even wearing his jacket, which meant he'd walked straight out the door and to the harbor when the news came.

I should have been grateful, I supposed. If there was one thing that was true about my uncle, it was that he'd never take his eye from me. There was no greater comfort. There was also no greater curse.

I stared at the hand he'd set on my shoulder, a wave of nausea gripping my belly. His knuckles were scraped, the skin torn. They were the marks of a fight. I was right, I thought. His was the hand that had struck Paj. His were the words that had poisoned the only good thing I'd ever had.

We walked the dark, empty street in tandem, like two limbs of the same body. The rain had stopped and the cobblestones gleamed, reflecting the streetlamps. I watched our shapes flash over their surfaces, swallowing hard. We looked like the same person.

My uncle didn't say a word. Not as we crossed under the archway of the harbor. Not as we stepped into Lower Vale. It wasn't until we were standing in front of the door to the house that he turned to me.

I lifted my chin, meeting his eyes, because that was what Henrik wanted. And I always gave him what he wanted.

"Do we need to clear the air?" he said evenly.

What was unbelievable about that moment was that he really wanted to. He'd done what he thought he had to, and now he wanted to make good about it. His head tilted to one side, as if measuring me. But there was a nothing left of me to size up.

"There comes a time in all our lives when we have to choose," he began. "It came for me, and now it's come for you. This family—this house—is first. You know that. And I know I can count on you to do what you have to."

He spoke with a father's tone, but there was venom dripping from the words. He wasn't asking.

"You could have talked to me about it," I said, my voice ragged. "Given me a chance to deal with it myself."

He nodded, as if giving me that much. "Maybe. You could have talked to me about it too."

Something flickered in the window above, and I glanced up as a shadow disappeared. Murrow and Ezra were probably waiting for us. The whole family was probably behind that door. I wondered if they'd all known where Henrik was going when he left the house for the docks. I wondered if they knew whose blood stained his hands when he'd returned.

"What did you think would happen when I found out you've been secretly seeing a trader for the last six months? Not just any trader. A trader from the *Scourge*," he said patiently. "You were sloppy, Auster. We don't get involved with jobs. We don't get involved, period. Not unless you have my approval. It's a system that protects all of us."

"Everyone in the family has people who warm their beds. Even you spend nights in a tavern."

"I don't think that's what was happening there," he replied, giving me a knowing look. "Now, if you want to admit that whatever you had going with that trader was more than a warm bed, that's another matter. That's another conversation entirely."

I'd seen members of our family go through that process before. My uncle Noel had done it when he brought Anthelia to family dinner for inspection. But bringing someone home to the Roths was a matter of bringing them into the fold. *If* they were accepted. When that happened, they became one of us. Same rules. Same expectations. Same consequences for not falling in line.

The worst thing I could do was tell Henrik how I felt about Paj, because it wasn't a body hunger or infatuation that kept me going back to see him every two weeks. It was a love. A deep, vicious love. If I told Henrik that when he'd gone down to the docks, he'd cut a part of me that would never heal, he would see it as a precarious weakness. More worrisome than that, he'd see it as a liability. And liabilities were never left lingering in our family.

"Well?" he said. "Which is it?"

In those few seconds of silence, the gaping wound inside of me bled until I couldn't feel any bit of warmth. The lie was my own death sentence. "It's nothing like that. Just a bit a fun that got out of hand."

Henrik frowned inquisitively. It didn't matter if he thought I was lying because he knew I wouldn't disobey him. I would never risk it because Paj would get a lot more than a broken nose if I did.

No, my uncle had won.

"You're right. I should have told you," I said.

He nodded, and with that, he let the door swing open. The pain inside of me grew teeth as I climbed the stairs, eating me from the inside out. It rippled beneath my skin, under the tailored jacket and the clean, crisp linen. But the tightly stitched seams I was made of were tearing open.

The candle in my room was lit when I came down the hallway. Murrow sat in the chair beside the window and Ezra stood against the wall. They said nothing as I came into the room.

They glanced at each other wordlessly as I sat down on the bed, unlacing my boots.

"Aus." Murrow finally spoke.

"Get the fuck out," I said, my voice on the verge of tears.

They obeyed without question. Without any words of comfort. What could they possibly say? We were all trapped in the same cage.

The door shut as I unbuttoned my vest and my shirt methodically, dropping them on the floor. I stared at them as the quiet house turned into a devouring beast around me, the walls closing in slowly until I felt as if I were being crushed between them.

When a broken cry escaped my throat, I picked up the pillow behind me and pressed my face into it. I wept, muffling the sound, with only the house as witness. I was born beneath this roof, and I would die here too.

Alone.

.˙.

ELEVEN

.˙.

The house of Roth was alive with voices.

As a kid, family dinners were my favorite time. My uncles would play with me, and my cousins and my aunt Eden would sit at the piano in the other room, filling the house with music. There was laughter and a blazing fire and enough rye to go around. But when it was time to eat, the business began. Tonight was no different.

I set Henrik's ledger beside his plate, where he liked it. Murrow and his father Casimir were already standing behind their chairs down the table. The rest of the family filed in, their chatter quieting as we waited for Henrik. He appeared a moment later, and it wasn't until he sat that the rest of us took our seats.

No one wasted any time, cutting into the roasted pig and passing the bread to fill our plates. When everyone was served, Henrik flipped open the ledger, calling the meeting to order.

He went down the list of inquiries—jobs, bribes, supplies, deals. One by one, the members of the family gave their reports and answered his questions as he scratched on the open page. Later, I'd do the sums and check them three times, like I did every week.

Things were back to normal. The same routines that had governed my existence for the last seventeen years were reset like broken bones, even if they were badly healed. Inside, I was empty. But outside, I was the groomed, respectful nephew I'd been raised to be. And Henrik had rewarded me for it. In the last six weeks, he'd given me more responsibility and entrusted me with tasks he usually reserved for my uncles. It wouldn't be long before I had my own stake—an arm of the family business to govern as my own.

There was a shift happening among the Roths. I'd seen it before, when my grandfather Felix promoted my uncles into roles of leadership. He'd chosen Henrik as his successor, and after he died, they went on with things the way they'd been taught. When Henrik was gone, someone else would take the chair in his study, and there wasn't a day that went by that I hoped it wouldn't be me.

"I need someone at the tavern tonight to keep an eye on the barkeep. I think he's dealing with someone else on his rye and I want to know who it is."

I kept my eyes pinned to my plate, not moving.

"I'll do it." Ezra volunteered without hesitation, shooting me a look. He and Murrow knew that on days when the *Scourge* would be docking in Bastian, I gave the tavern a wide berth.

"All right," Henrik said, picking up his knife to take a bite of pork off the tip of the blade. "What else?"

Noel set down his fork and wiped his mouth with his napkin. "There's a sailmaker in Holland's ranks named Leo who says she's ordered two sets of clipper sails. I think she's adding to the fleet again."

Henrik grunted, thinking. He hated the gem merchant Holland almost as much as he hated the guilds, and it seemed every other month she was commissioning new ships. "When are they due?"

"Two weeks."

"How much did you pay him?"

"Two hundred and fifty coppers."

Henrik wrote the number down. "Can you find out what ports they'll be scheduled for and what the inventory will be?"

"I have people who will talk for coin." Casimir jumped in.

"Good. Fool probably thinks she'll finally get that permit to trade in Ceros." He tsked. "Auster, I need you to go up to the smith's pier and pick up a package."

I nodded in answer, still chewing.

"You can do the numbers later."

The ledger finally closed a half hour later, and the family was dismissed. Everyone lingered in the kitchen over a game of Three Widows, but I pulled on my cap and left for the pier. The orderly chaos of family dinner made me thankful for the solitary task. I walked with my hands in my pockets, watching the windows and rooftops every twelve steps. I didn't even mean to do it anymore. I was so used to the habit that it had become, a voice that constantly ran in the back of my mind, counting.

When I reached the top of the hill that overlooked the harbor, I didn't dare turn. The only thing that had kept my heart beating the last six weeks was never allowing myself to know if Paj's ship had definitely come in. That way, I couldn't think about how close he was. I couldn't be tempted to go and find him.

I kept walking until I reached the sixth building, the smith's pier. Henrik always had dealings with the smiths because they were least reputable of the guilds. They kept him supplied with the tools he needed, and he kept them stocked with information on the other guilds. It was a fair trade.

I knocked on the metal door and leaned into the jamb, glancing back to the street, where people were coming and going with crates and carts. When it opened, the smith's daughter frowned. Her blonde hair was braided back from her face and her hands were covered in what looked like liquid charcoal. "Oh. It's you." She disapproved of her father's partnership with Henrik and I didn't blame her.

"Good day to you, too." I muttered.

She sighed, pointing an elbow at the corner, where a package wrapped in brown paper was waiting for me. "Over there." She held her black-stained hands up in front of her as an excuse for making me get it myself.

I glared at her, pushing inside the door to pick it up. "A pleasure, as always." I smiled sarcastically, tipping my cap to her before I went back outside.

The door slammed behind me and I tucked the package under my arm, starting back up the path. But I stopped short when I looked up from the cobblestones to the corner.

Everything on the street seemed to freeze midmotion around me as I stared at him.

Paj stood beneath an unlit streetlamp ahead, the wind catching his shirt and pulling it around the shape of him. He met my eyes before he tipped his head in the direction of the alley and disappeared into it.

My gaze immediately went to the rooftops, then the windows, before finally falling to both sides of the street. I had no reason to believe Henrik was having me watched, but that's what I'd thought six weeks ago. If I turned down that alley, I was taking the chance that I was wrong.

I clenched my teeth, thinking. Around the corner, the alley called me toward it. I couldn't keep walking if I wanted to.

My grip on the package tightened. I turned, following the narrow path between the buildings. Bolted doors lined the two piers, and I could see the toes of Paj's boots sticking out in the alley where the next one was set into the brick. I took a deep breath before I reached it.

He stood beneath the overhang, one shoulder leaned into the door. The shadows carved his face in deep grooves beneath his cheekbones. I swallowed hard, staring at him.

"Hey," he said, then pressed his lips together.

I looked both ways down the alley before I stepped up and put myself on the other side of the doorway, where we couldn't be seen.

He squared his shoulders to mine and his eyes ran over me slowly, making me feel like every bone in my body was unhinging itself. "How are you?"

But I couldn't speak. There was no breath in my lungs. And I wasn't going to start lying. Not now.

I was angry with him. And angry with myself. But I also wanted to touch him so badly that my hand curled into a fist inside of my jacket pocket.

Paj didn't seem to mind the silence. He never did. His face was healed, but I thought I could see the slightest curve to his nose that hadn't been there before.

"Did you follow me?" I finally asked.

He nodded. "From the house."

I hadn't seen him. But then again, if anyone knew how to stay out of my notice, it was Paj. He had my habits memorized.

"I wanted to see you," he said. "I mean . . . I wanted to see you, but I came to talk."

My brow furrowed, a tiny alarm inside of me going off. "What's wrong?"

"Nothing," he answered, looking nervous. His eyes went to the alley. "I have a question to ask you."

"All right," I said apprehensively.

Paj's chest expanded as he drew in a slow breath. It took him a moment to let it go. "What if I had a way for you to leave Bastian?"

The alarm inside of me was a high-pitched wailing now. "What?"

"What if I had a way for us to leave. Would you come with me?"

Us. The sound of it was like a thousand knives in my

gut. My mind skipped over the flood of thoughts, the waters parting around that one word. "What are you talking about?"

"I heard at the tavern that there's someone looking to be smuggled out of the city. They'll pay good coin."

"But . . ." I looked at him, shocked and puzzled at the same time.

"I'm going to put him in a crate and have it loaded into the cargo hull. He's going to pay me half tonight and half when we get to Ceros."

I shook my head. "Tell him to find someone else."

"It's enough coin for us to leave. Together."

"And go where?" The words came out harsh.

Paj met my eyes. "The Narrows."

The Narrows. Those waters were like the older but smaller and more sinister brother of the Unnamed Sea.

"The stryker on the *Scourge* is a friend," he continued, hardly taking a breath. "He's agreed to take you on so that the helmsman won't ask questions and when we get to Ceros, I'll leave my post on the ship."

This wasn't a fleeting thought. He had a plan and, from the sound of it, he'd put it together in only the last few hours. "What if you get caught?"

He shrugged. "I won't."

But this wasn't part of Paj's skillset. He was a deckhand, not a smuggler. He didn't know the first thing about running jobs. He didn't even know how to lie.

"Paj." Even saying his name hurt. "You're not doing this."

"I'm doing it whether you say yes or no," he answered. "The next time I'm in Bastian will be the last time, Auster."

"What?" My heart was beating so hard that it felt like it might stop altogether.

He stared at my boots. "I'm leaving Bastian, with or without you."

"Why?"

"Because I can't ever come back here if I can't be with you."

The image of him wavered in my vision as I tried to blink the tears back.

"Henrik might run things in Lower Vale, but he's no one in Ceros. We can join up on a crew or take on apprenticeships somewhere. But you have be done with the Roths. Completely."

Even the idea was like a snake coiling inside of me. Leaving was more complicated than that. Bastian was all I'd ever known. I hadn't been places, like Paj. I didn't know how to crew a ship or find work. And if I left the family, I wouldn't ever be able to come back. There were some sins Henrik would never forgive, and that was one of them.

"I meant what I said. I love you. I don't want to be without you." He paused, the sound of his voice taking on an ache. "But I also meant it when I said that I can't do this anymore."

I stared at him wordlessly. I wanted to say yes. But if I did, I wouldn't be the only one who'd become an enemy of the Roths. Paj would too. That wasn't a decision I could make lightly.

"Let me do this for you. Please," he breathed.

I searched his eyes. Paj was tough and he was smart, but he wasn't built for this kind of work. I sorted through the pieces in my mind, organizing them the way I would if I were planning a job. If he didn't do this right, he was going to get himself killed. "Cut the stryker in on the coin to keep him quiet. I don't care if he's your friend—copper is the most efficient form of loyalty. And collect from this guy, whoever he is, *before* you let him off the ship in Ceros."

"You still haven't said yes," he said, and suddenly, he looked afraid of my answer.

A metal door creaked open down the alley, followed by footsteps. We both went still, listening. They were coming in our direction.

"In two weeks, I'll be waiting for you at the docks before the first harbor bell." Paj lowered his voice. He stepped forward so that his feet were staggered between mine and as soon as I caught his scent, I inhaled it deep inside me. He touched his lips to mine gently, opening them just enough to taste me, and I curled my hand into his jacket.

The footsteps grew louder and he broke away from me just as a tear crossed the bridge of his nose. "I'll see you."

His jacket slipped from my clenched fingers as he stepped out into the alley and vanished.

I stared at the brick where he'd stood only moments ago, and a man passed the opening with a stack of wood propped on his shoulder. I waited for him to reach the end of the pier before I finally stepped out, walking in the opposite direction that Paj had gone. And I could feel it—the pain in my chest as he drew further from me. Like a thread tied between my ribs, pulling.

I wasn't sure I could live like that forever.

TWELVE

I sat at the writing desk in front of the window with one hand stuck in my hair, scribbling in the ledger by candlelight. The numbers streamed through my mind like the notes of a song as the sound of voices downstairs rumbled. My uncles and cousins were still sitting around the fire, but Henrik wanted the sums done before the end of the day, and I'd taken my leave gratefully, eager for the quiet.

There was always work to do and there was little rest in the house, but on the nights when I did the math in my uncle's ledger, it did feel something like rest. I'd sit in the dim, quiet room with the birds outside the window, and kept company by the sound of the quill on the thick parchment. It was the only time I wasn't worrying or thinking about anything except for the numbers.

I finished the sums after the third count and closed the book with a snap, stretching my arms over my head. The sun was finally setting and it cloaked my room in darkness, making it colder. The warmth of the fire drifted up the stairs as I came down them with the ledger tucked under my arm, and I crossed the hall into my uncle's study, setting the book on his desk. There it would wait until morning.

I looked around the small room, where portraits of the Roths were hung on the walls. I knew all their names because I'd been told their stories. Mine hung below my father's, my likeness encased in a round carved frame. I met my own eyes for a moment before I slipped back into the hall and made my way toward the kitchen, where my family was still tangled in conversation. But when I passed the open door of the workshop, I stopped, catching my hand on the doorframe.

The glow of the forge lit the corner of the long, rectangular room, where Ezra's silhouette was carved into its light. The roof was made of large, tiled panes of glass that slanted down to one side, and they were covered in a film of soot from the chimneys of Lower Vale and moss from the damp air. But the workshop had a smell that was nostalgic to me. It was the smell of home.

Ezra pulled on thick gloves and fetched the crucible from the fire, carefully lowering it to the mold on the table. I watched from the shadows as he poured the shimmering melted silver in a stream. It gleamed like liquid sunlight. When he set it down, he pulled off the gloves and dropped them to the table.

I came to stand beside him, staring at the mold. "Knife?" I asked.

Beads of sweat lined his forehead from the heat of the forge. "Yeah. A gift for some guild member or something."

He said it without any resentment. Ezra didn't complain when he was asked to do things, which is one of the reasons Henrik liked him.

"I never thanked you," I said, leaning into the table beside him.

"For what?"

"For that day at the gem merchant's."

Ezra's eyes slid to meet mine. "You'd have done the same for me," he said, as if it were the most normal thing in the world to kill a man to protect the people you loved. And he did love me. I'd always known that.

We'd guessed he was a about year or two younger than me, though Ezra wasn't sure of his exact age, and he always treated me like a brother. And he was right. If it had been the other way around, I would have drawn my knife too.

"Thank you anyway." I smirked.

He smiled back, and it was a rare thing to see. Ezra was always so serious.

I shoved his elbow with mine and left him to his work. The loud ping of his mallet rang out as I went down the hallway, and as soon as I came into the kitchen, a glass of rye was shoved into my hand. I stood in the corner beside a tipsy Murrow and watched as my uncles played dice, their laughter growing louder by the hour. When the last of them had finally trailed up to their rooms, I threw Murrow's arm over my shoulder and lugged him up the stairs. He stumbled alongside me, still chuckling at something Noel had said, and when I dumped him into his bed, he instantly fell asleep.

I laughed, yanking the shoes from his feet and lining them up beside the door so they could be shined for the morning. The house of Roth was like clockwork, even in this—drunk bastards being thrown into bed.

I looked down at him as he snored and closed the door behind me, then went to my own room. It was a long time before I heard Ezra come up the stairs for the night and close his door. His work often stretched into the late hours, and he didn't mind because he liked the empty workshop.

I lay in bed awake with one arm tucked behind my head and a hand on my chest. It rose and fell evenly, and I realized that my heart was beating softly. Slowly. The pinch that usually twisted there was gone, and I breathed in a smooth rhythm. With every hour that passed, it seemed to grow calmer, until the very farthest reach of the sky was barely lit with the sunrise.

I stood in front of the mirror and took the pocket watch from my vest. It clicked as I opened it one last time, rubbing a thumb over the face before I set it down on the table softly. The dresser scraped as I moved it away from the wall, and I reached behind it to the opening in the back of the drawer. Inside, a small purse of coin was waiting. I dropped it into my pocket and chose the least expensive of my jackets before I unlatched the window and let it swing open to the night.

The street was silent below and I crept out onto the roof, perching myself on its edge. I waited, listening for footsteps before I leapt to the ground.

My feet hit the cobblestones and I stood, brushing off my trousers as I looked up. My room was dark, but my hands froze in midair when my eyes landed on the next window. There was no light coming from Ezra's room, but a white gleam was framed behind the glass. His shirt. I couldn't see his face, but he stood there, completely still, watching me.

I swallowed hard, waiting to see what he would do. But when he reached up and closed his window, he disappeared, and the faint glow of the candle was snuffed out. A sad smile pulled at my lips as I turned my back on the house and started walking. And I didn't stop until the harbor was in view.

The streetlamps were orbs of light floating in the air over the harbor. Below, the ships drifted like ghosts on the mist-covered sea. I was a ghost too—the only thing awake in the sleeping city, and, for the rest of my life, I would remember that moment as the most peace I had ever felt.

In the distance, the *Scourge* sat on the still water, a few lanterns on the deck already lit. In their glow, I could see him. Standing at the railing and watching the harbor's entrance. He was waiting for me. And if there were any doubt lurking in my mind, it vanished when the smile pulled at my lips. The blood in my veins would always be Roth, but my heart belonged to Paj.

I took the steps down to the dock, into the thick fog, letting it swallow me up.

And just like that, I was gone.

DRIFT

ONE

This ship is going to sink.

    The thought echoed in my mind each time I swung the adze, driving plug after plug into the hull of the *Featherback*. The ship rocked against a wave, and I propped my feet against the wood to keep the sling that held me still. The ropes suspended from the deck's railing above creaked as I waited for the water to settle.

    Out of habit, I checked the horizon for any sign of a storm. But the sky was blue and clear, the sun hot on my shoulders. It wouldn't so much as rain today, and that was good. The roof on the new merchant's house wasn't complete yet, and we couldn't afford to miss any trade. Not when we were still trying to convince helmsmen that a stop at Jeval was worth the day it cost them on their route to or from the Unnamed Sea.

    I dropped the adze back into my belt. "Ailee! Pitch!"

    The girl's small frame moved like a scurrying mouse on the dock below as she made her way to the anchored line that controlled the bucket of hanging above me. With quick hands, she lowered it, and when she was sure I could reach it comfortably, she re-tied the line. Her cropped, curly black hair blew across her face as she looked up at me, waiting for my next instruction.

This was the third time the *Featherback* had docked at Jeval needing to be patched, and by my estimation, the next storm would finish her. It wouldn't be the first vessel I'd worked on to sink since opening up for business, and it wouldn't be the last. Crews like this one knew their time was running out— they just wanted to rack up every copper they could before it happened. There were enough arrogant bastards in the Narrows to think that when the vessel succumbed to its fate, that they'd be spared.

The stink of the black pitch in the hanging bucket beside me burned in my nose as I took up the swab and painted it over the last plug.

"What'ya say, Willa?" the helmsman called out from below. He peered up at me, squinting, Ailee posted dutifully at his side.

"Hard to say." I returned the swab to its bucket, reaching for the knotted lines behind me. In a series of movements I had memorized, I unlocked the pulley and lowered myself down.

He stepped aside when I made it to the dock and I caught hold of the post, pulling myself in. My legs were half asleep from hanging in the sling so long. I could hardly feel the hot wood planks under my feet.

Ailee was waiting with her hands extended as I unfastened the heavy tool belt and draped it over her shoulder. Her curls danced around her sharply cut jaw, her pale blue eyes rimmed in thick black lashes. Two months ago, that face had been hollow, her skin pallid. Now, she was sun-kissed, her bony frame less gaunt. She was small for eleven years old, but that would serve her well as a bosun. Only in the last few days had she stopped swaying under my belt's weight, and I could see the first signs of strength taking shape in her arms and shoulders. Before long, she'd be able to hoist herself up on the lines.

"Bag's empty." I nodded to the canvas pouch that had held the wooden cone plugs. "And the adze needs sharpening."

She gave a quick nod, turning on her heel and disappearing up the dock.

"Well?" The helmsman waited.

I looked up to the *Featherback* one last time. The hull was spotted with patches from stern to bow.

Yeah. This ship was *definitely* going to sink.

"Stay out of the shallows, even when the winds aren't too high," I said. "One scrape and that hull will breach. I'd also keep anything valuable you're trading fitted with floats and tied down up on the decks. That cargo hold is a disaster waiting to happen."

His mouth twisted to one side, but he eventually nodded. The man wasn't a fool. "All right. What do I owe ya?"

I pulled the ledger from where it was tucked into the back of my pants, flipping through the wrinkled pages. "That's eleven shot plugs, the pitch, the work . . ." I did the math in my head. "Forty-two coppers should do it."

The helmsman was already pulling one of the coin purses

from his belt. He counted, mouth moving silently around the numbers.

Behind him, the harbor was busy. Nine of the fourteen bays were filled with everything from schooners to cutters to a large brig from Ceros stopping on its way to Sagsay Holm. The Jevalis hadn't been happy when Koy showed up with me and my coin to launch a port on their island, and they hadn't let me forget it. But there was no denying the transformation underway on Jeval.

When I'd first arrived, there'd been only dredgers hocking pyre on these docks, with the exception of a few women selling guinea fowl eggs and kids trading polished abalone shells for scraps of food. Now, there were hucksters who walked the bays with Jevali-made palm rope and island-forged iron riggings that every ship had need for. There was even a young sailmaker who'd left the island and apprenticed in Sowan and was now setting up shop next to my post.

It had been almost seven months since we finished the new docks that encircled the barrier islands, and the first opening bell of the merchant's house had rung just six weeks ago. There was only room enough for twelve stalls inside, and not all of them were even filled most days, but in another year, it would be a different story.

"There you go." The helmsman dropped the purse into my hand and I nodded, tucking it into my vest.

The feeling had come back into my legs, but my stomach was already twisting with hunger. Even so, it would be hours before I got a chance to sit down and have a meal.

I snaked through the bodies on the docks, headed for the brig in the distance. The ship's crew members were quadruple those of the other vessels that docked here, which meant there was copper on its way into a lot of Jevali pockets. It was the second time the well-known *Iris* had docked, and with luck, the helmsman would spread the word about the growing enterprise we were building. As long as the Jevalis didn't do anything to muck it up before they left.

I shouldered past the crowd of dredgers waiting in line at the merchant's house and found my way to the end of the harbor, where Fret set up his makeshift stall each morning. He sat on an overturned barrel behind a little wooden table that was littered with rare seashells and bits of valuable coral.

"Any luck today?" I asked, leaning against the post. I kept my distance, eyes on the highest rise of the island. It was in both our best interests not to draw attention to our arrangement.

"Here and there," he rasped. "Never underestimate the power of a good story, Willa. It can sell the most worthless piece of junk to any fool."

I smirked. He had a knack for conjuring up old sea tales about a rusted piece of metal from a famed ship or a mythical creature who'd lost a tooth. There was at least one bastard a day who gave in to temptation and bought whatever he was selling.

"Anything else of note?" I asked.

His bottom lip jutted out as he thought. "Other than the number of times I've heard your name mentioned in somewhat unsavory conversation?"

"Yes," I exhaled, "other than that."

"Then, no. Nothing of note."

I scanned the docks, eyes flitting from one sun-leathered body to the next. I hadn't been able to win the Jevalis over, but that didn't stop them from making coin on the docks I'd helped to build. If it weren't for me and my copper, the island would still be living off of its dwindling caches of pyre.

My eyes stopped on a face I recognized. Bruin.

He stood at the corner of bay three, hands tucked into his pockets as he watched a cluster of the brig's crew coming down the docks. There was something about that look in his eye that made me follow his gaze. He was looking past the deckhands, to a woman with a coil of rope slung over her shoulder. She fell into step behind the crew, catching up in just a few seconds, and then Bruin was moving, folding himself into the crowd from the opposite direction.

As soon as he was weaving in and out of them, the woman lurched forward, tripping and throwing her arms out to catch herself on the man in front of her. Not just any man. The stryker of the *Iris*. He went toppling down and then Bruin was hoisting him up, back onto his feet. A string of words I couldn't hear passed between them as he brushed off the man's jacket and clapped him on the back. But the shine of gold clutched in his hand made me grit my teeth.

"Shit," I muttered, taking off in their direction.

The crew was already at the end of the docks, heading up the steps that led to the tavern by the time Bruin tucked that gold into his pocket.

I was only steps away when a hand caught me by the shoulder, twisting me around. Koy had hold of my vest, his attention on the end of the docks as he led me in the opposite direction.

"Don't even think about it." His voice was low, but his face was cast in a calm, unbothered expression.

I shrugged him off, whirling to face him. "I just watched Bruin pickpocket the *Iris*'s stryker."

If Koy was surprised, he didn't show it. There wasn't the slightest shift in the way he looked down at me. He was a whole head taller, maybe more, and his once long black hair was now cut almost to the scalp. Beneath one arm, he was carrying a crate filled with messages that had come in on one of the ships.

"Did you hear what I just said?"

He looked bored. "I did."

"How long do you think it's going to take him to realize his pocket watch is gone?" I flung a hand into the air.

"People are pickpocketed at every port, Willa."

"*We're* not every port. Every trader in the Narrows already thinks this island is nothing but a squatting place for thieves. If we want ships to keep docking here, to pick us up on their routes, we can't play into that story."

His eyes lifted over my head, to the bays behind me. "Doesn't look like it's keeping them away."

"Do you see a single crest from the Unnamed Sea in this harbor? It's not enough to plug holes for low-level traders. If we want Jeval to become a real port, we need the Saltbloods,"

109

I said, exasperated. "If we don't have their coin, then we don't have inventory. We don't have merchants or piers. We'll never have a drydock—"

Koy sighed, pinching the bridge of his nose between his eyes. "If I have to hear about this drydock one more time," he muttered.

"I'm telling you we need one. Only two other ports in the Narrows have them and we're the last stop before Sagsay Holm."

"There are about a hundred other things we need before that, Willa."

"We have a whole island just waiting to become a port city, Koy. And it's never going to happen if Jeval's reputation doesn't change."

"I told you. You have to pick your battles with them. We were living a life here long before you arrived, and things aren't going to change overnight."

"It's been almost a year, and I didn't just *arrive* here. I didn't wash up on that beach one day—you and I have a business agreement. We're partners."

"I know." His tone changed, softening. "I know that."

We'd had this conversation more times than I could count, and I knew that he agreed with me. Koy was the first person to see the potential of this place, but he was still stuck between the boy who'd grown up surviving here and the man he was trying to become—harbor master of the port of Jeval.

"I know it's not your strong suit, but you need to be patient," he said. "This is going to take time."

I glared at him. That, he wasn't wrong about. I'd never been good at waiting for anything, and it had gotten me into trouble more than once. But I also didn't want to fail at what we were doing here. In five years' time, we could be the first port of call for the ships from the Unnamed Sea who were coming to trade in the Narrows. The first gateway. That wasn't nothing.

His gaze went behind me and I looked back to see Ailee. She ducked under elbows, turning sideways to wedge herself between the crush of people. She still had my toolbelt draped over her shoulders like a sash, a new, full bag of shot plugs in one hand, my adze cradled protectively in the other.

"What is she still doing here?" Koy sighed.

"I told you, she's my apprentice."

He rolled his eyes. "And which one of us is paying to feed her?"

I narrowed my eyes at him. "I am."

"Good."

He started back up the docks and I watched him go. Ailee cowered a little as she passed him, getting impossibly smaller until he was out of sight. When she reached me, she was already rattling off the orders for the next ship on the docket.

"Bay nine, the little sloop with the red mainsail. Helmsman says the bilge pump is shot." She let the toolbelt slide from her shoulders into my hands.

I fastened it around me. "Please tell me it's not made of bronze."

"Wood." She smiled.

"What else?"

"Should have time for the schooner in bay one. I told him he'd have to wait until morning, just in case."

I nodded. "All right. Let's go."

"Oh!" She reached into her jacket pocket, pulling out a wad of cloth. "Here."

She set the small bundle into my hand and I unwrapped it to see a small hunk of cheese cut from the round in my post and an apple. I looked up at her.

"Haven't seen you eat today," she said, eyes bright.

The first time I saw her, I'd seen my brother. She was skin and bones, climbing down the ladder of a ship with a rusted scraper clenched in her teeth. For a month, each time that ship docked in our harbor, she climbed out like a rat to clean the hull before scuttling back in. It was a job for a grown deckhand, not an eleven-year-old girl, much less one that looked like she hadn't seen sunlight in weeks.

I knew what it looked like when a waterside stray was being starved in the belly of a ship, because I'd seen those signs in West. Every few weeks, he made port in Ceros long enough to give me and our mother a few coppers he'd earned, and each time he showed up, he was sicker. Weaker. That all changed the day he came home and said that he'd taken a place on a crew for a trader named Saint—the best and worst thing that ever happened to him. To us.

The irony wasn't lost on me. I'd left the *Marigold* and West to finally sever the binds that kept us beholden to each other. Yet, here I was, tying myself to the first person I saw who reminded me of him.

I looked down at the apple and cheese in my hands.

The day I offered to wave the ship repair fees in exchange for that helmsman to leave Ailee behind in Jeval, I'd known, deep down, what I was doing. There was part of me that needed someone to take care of. But worse than that, there was also a part that needed someone to take care of *me*.

‹›‹

TWO

‹›‹

S peck's tavern wasn't really a tavern at all. Not yet anyway. The only part of the harbor that sat between the barrier islands and the beach was a series of narrow planks that stretched out over the water. They led to one place—a crude structure that was still mid-build, with a palm thatch roof and no walls to speak of. It didn't have the dark, lamplit glow of the taverns in the other port cities, but that seemed prudent given the track record of the Jevalis. Even in the wild, somewhat lawless waters of the Narrows, there were certain rules. But here, people took what they wanted, and I preferred to feel like I could keep my eye on them, even if that was just a lie I told myself.

I followed the planks, my back aching from the work on the bilge pump. Ailee had been right. I'd had time for the schooner, too, which meant more copper before sundown. It also meant I'd need a glass of rye to curb the pain that settled between my shoulder blades. Otherwise, I'd never sleep.

The tavern was also the only place on the island that could

pass as an inn. Four shanties had been constructed at the end of four separate docks and at high tide, especially on windy days, the water rose close enough to sometimes slosh in through the open door. It was a luxury Koy had fought me on, and the fact that they hadn't gotten much use yet only served to prove his point. The other dredgers who'd formed a kind of council agreed with him. The only purpose they really served was to oppose me, though they'd also been useful in organizing building crews for the docks. Still, the shanties had been a strike against me that even I couldn't argue with.

The chairs and tables were mostly full beneath the canopy, and a few peals of laughter carried away on the wind. I was beginning to recognize faces among the ship crews, and that was a very good sign. Helmsmen were coming back, even when they weren't made destitute by a storm or a cargo hold of beetles ruining their grain stores.

"There she is." Speck stopped wiping the wood counter when he caught sight of me.

The sun had just fallen behind the almost-mountain that crested the island, making the water reflect pink and orange around us. In this light, even Speck looked like a decently fed and watered creature. He smiled as he set a rye glass down in front of me and took a bottle from beneath the counter. He didn't wait for my copper before he poured.

I took one of the stools, studying the tables along the edge of the docks. I didn't see the stryker of the brig, but if there'd been a scene about the missing pocket watch, I'd hear about it soon enough.

"Where's the kid?" Speck asked, setting his elbows on the bar.

"Sleeping."

She'd been out cold before I'd even gotten my tools cleaned, curling up in her hammock only seconds after she'd finished her porridge. We'd had it every night for the last two weeks because that was all I could afford, but she hadn't once complained.

"How are you doing on rye?" I asked.

"Been runnin' low, but Koy put in the order with that helmsman headed to Sowan. Should be here in a few days and we have enough to last 'til then."

I stared into my glass, rubbing my temples with my fingers. If it wasn't one thing, it was another. If I wanted my drydock, then we needed more coin. In order to get it, we had to have more ships docking. But the more crew we had in this harbor, the more rye we needed for them to drink. It was a delicate ecosystem that needed constant management and attention. I hated to admit it, but Koy happened to be very good at that.

A body sat down on the stool next to me, and Raef's ring-clad hand tapped the counter beside my elbow. I turned my head toward him, the pain between my shoulder blades now creeping up my neck.

Koy's brother looked like he'd just come in off a dive. White, wayward trails of salt crusted the hair on his arms, his pants still wet. His black hair was even longer than Koy's was when I first met him, but Raef was a few years younger and had a softness to his face. It put people at ease, and that had come in handy when he was one of the only Jevalis on the island who didn't want to see me tied to the reef.

"You look like shit." He smiled up one side of his face, making him twice as handsome.

"Thanks."

Speck poured him a glass and Raef turned on the stool to face the tavern. He'd told me once that he'd never left the island. Not in his entire life. Looking at him now, with that sunset on his dark skin and the sea wind in his hair, I couldn't imagine him anyplace else.

He drank the rye in two swallows. "How'd it go with the schooner?"

"Shipworm," I said, flatly.

He raised an eyebrow at me. "Let me guess, something you'd be able to fix with—"

"A drydock!" I cut him off, groaning.

He and Speck met eyes, both burying smiles.

"If we had a drydock, I'd have ships from every port fighting for one of those bays out there."

Speck frowned. "Well, we wouldn't have enough rye for them all. I can tell you that much."

I glowered at him. "I need you to talk to Koy, Raef. Make him see reason."

It wasn't the first time I'd tried to use Raef as a go-between, something he didn't appreciate. But I didn't have much choice when Koy wouldn't listen to me.

The sound of a coin purse drew our attention down the counter, where a group of Jevalis crowded around the last few stools. When I saw the purse, I followed the hand beside it to its owner. Bruin.

"A bottle, Speck." He was grinning smugly, his chin lifted.

He'd probably hocked the stryker's pocket watch before the merchant house's closing bell. Now he was going to blow it all on a bottle of rye we couldn't spare just so he could do it all over again tomorrow.

I slid off my stool and Raef immediately caught my arm, holding me in place. "Not a good idea, Willa."

I tore myself from his grip, shoving through the Jevalis until I reached Bruin. He stood so much taller than my own height that he had to step backward just to look at me.

"Speck," I said, eyes still fixed on Bruin, "don't touch that bottle."

Bruin laughed. "What?"

"That coin's going back to the stryker. You can buy your own rye."

Bruin stepped closer and the crowd around us drifted back. "Willa . . ."

I could hear the warning from Raef, but I ignored him. Behind the counter, Speck's gaze jupmed from me to Bruin.

"That's *my* copper," Bruin said, voice lowering.

"No. It's not. I've told you before, all of you, that stealing will get you barred from these docks. Permanently."

His smile widened. "And how exactly do you think you're going to make that happen?"

Half the tavern had taken notice now. I could feel dozens of eyes on me.

Bruin's stare didn't break from mine as I lifted my hand. I didn't hesitate before I snatched up the coin purse, turning on my heel. But a second later, his shadow was moving on the floor beside me.

I sank down and slid to the side as I reached to the back of my belt, pulling my dagger free, and as I pivoted, it lifted between us. The sunset glinted off the jewels set into its hilt, making tiny purple and red flecks of light dance up my arm.

The tip of the blade was pointed at Bruin's chest, and that was enough to push him over the edge. His fist raised up, ready to come down on me when I was suddenly pulled out of reach. I nearly fell, toppling into the table beside me and knocking over two chairs.

Koy was standing between us, his tall frame matching Bruin's.

Anyone in the tavern who hadn't been watching us was staring now, the eyes of the ship crews lit with the anticipation of a tavern brawl. But Koy looked placid, his calm exterior intact. He squared his shoulders to Bruin, giving me his back.

"You should talk to your girl about taking what doesn't belong to her." Bruin's eyes cut to me.

Your girl.

My blood boiled. That's what they called me when they wanted to humiliate me in front of Koy, but I hadn't seen him react to it once. The Jevalis didn't seem to get under his skin the way they did mine. If they did, he was good at not showing it.

"Speck." Koy's even, steady tone was the same it always

was. "Give him his bottle. He can drink his rye on the beach tonight."

Bruin's head tilted a little to one side, sizing Koy up. Koy was always finding a compromise, and the Jevalis didn't like it. They were in a constant game of trying to make Koy choose between me and them, and so far, he'd managed to avoid the trap.

Speck obeyed, taking one of the unopened bottles and sliding it across the counter. Bruin stared at Koy for another long moment before he took it and stalked out, the others on his heels.

The rest of the tavern begrudgingly went back to their drinks, and Koy watched them go as I slid the dagger back into my belt. When he turned, he didn't face me. He was looking at Raef. "What did I tell you?"

Raef's hands lifted into the air in front of him, mock innocence on his face. "Hey, I tried," he said, looking to Speck for back up. "Right? Didn't I try?"

Speck, the only one smart enough to keep his mouth shut, didn't say a word.

"What do you mean, *what did I tell you*?" I looked between the brothers. "Koy?"

He ignored me, snatching the coin purse from my hand and tossing it onto the counter in front of Speck. "I told you to leave it."

"And I told *you*, we can't run things like this. Not unless we want it all to fall apart."

Koy shook his head. "You don't understand how things work here. I do. Would it kill you to listen to me?"

"Would it kill *you* to listen to *me*?"

Raef drained his glass, attempting to slip away unnoticed.

"Did he tell you to watch me?" I said, stopping him. "Is that it?"

Raef shot a panicked look in Koy's direction.

"You've got to be kidding me," I muttered, raking a hand over my face. "So, what? You have your brother keeping watch over me now?"

"Believe me, it's the last thing I should have to do," Koy shot back.

"No one asked you to. I don't need you watching out for me. I can take care of myself."

"Really?" He took a step closer, voice lowering. "Then what's this?"

Before I realized what he was going to do, his hand touched my face, rough fingers grazing over the scar that marked my cheek.

I recoiled, putting several feet between us. My hand instinctively went to the scar, the words striking deep. It felt as if the air had been sucked from my lungs, the shame of it burning beneath my skin.

I could feel the sting of traitorous tears in my eyes as I stared at Koy, but I breathed through it, refusing to be the first to look away. The regret was already there in his expression, some form of an apology folded in the way he was staring back at me.

"Uh, Willa?" Speck's voice was no more than an echo at the back of my mind.

I'd caught Koy staring at the scar more than once, but he'd never said anything about it. In fact, he was the only person who hadn't. And now he wanted to dangle it between us like a counterweight to an argument?

"*Willa,*" Speck said again, the nervous sound of the words finally pulling my gaze from Koy.

Behind the counter, Speck's eyes were wide. He was staring out past the barrier islands.

I moved past Koy to the edge of the dock, squinting at the shape of a ship drifting into the harbor. It was a brig, but even larger than the one already docked, and it had three towering masts with a carved bow in the shape of a draped, floral garland.

"Is that . . . ?" Raef's words sputtered out as the ship turned just enough for us to see the gloss of the wood. The crisp white sails. Even the bowsprit was tipped in bronze.

This wasn't a Narrows-born trader or a Narrows-built ship. This vessel hailed from the Unnamed Sea.

THREE

I didn't sleep.

By the time the sun was rising and the seabirds were calling out over the water, I was up, pacing the floor of my post in an anxious pattern that had Ailee staring at me. She was sitting in her hammock, toes brushing the wood planks as she gently swung.

"Should we . . . go out there?" she asked, eyes moving again to the door.

I bit down on my thumbnail, watching through the window. The brig from the Unnamed Sea had dropped anchor after dark and the only sign of the crew was the coin master who'd come down to pay three nights' docking fee. Koy had done well and played it cool, marking down the ship as if it were any other. But when he met my eyes over the woman's head, they held everything I was thinking. That *this* was our chance.

"We wait." I said.

"And what exactly are we waiting for?" Ailee tried again.

123

"If they're staying three nights, they most likely need some kind of repairs, but waiting on the dock like a beggar isn't the right move. Letting the helmsman know how desperate we are for business will only invite them to take advantage of us. Remember that."

Ailee nodded, her expression seriouse.

"You can't trust these Satlblood bastards."

"So, we want them here. We just don't want them to *know* we want them here," she said.

"Exactly."

She still looked confused, but she didn't press it. She swung in the hammock, fingers tapping her knees until we finally heard footsteps on the dock outside.

I stopped pacing, meeting her eyes as she sat up. We were silent for several seconds before a knock sounded on the door.

I crossed the small room as Ailee unhooked one side of her hammock and let it fall to the floor. Then she lowered the counter latched to the wall beneath the window, and in an instant, the little room was transformed from a hovel to a post.

Koy stood on the other side of the door when I opened it, his ship roster propped on one arm. "Ship in bay twelve is asking for the bosun."

I let out a tight breath, giving him a nod.

"You ready?" he asked.

There was still the hint of that apology in his eyes from when he'd embarrassed me last night, but his nerves were as shaky as mine. A lot could hinge on this. If the helmsman had a good experience, he'd likely return. He may even spread the word about the small but economical port developing in the wide stretch of barren water that connected the Narrows and the Unnamed Sea. If he *didn't* have a good experience, that information would travel, too.

I fell into step beside him and Ailee followed.

"Ship's name is the *Wellworthy*. Port of origin is Bastian, the helmsman's name is Dennon. My guess is they trade mainly jewelry and gems, that kind of thing."

"And their route?"

Koy scanned the docks around us as we walked. "That's the strange part. They're not on a regular route. I got a glance at the navigator's logs when he was marking coordinates and it looks like they've been stopping at every port there is. Ship's riding light in the water so I don't think they've got much inventory."

"So, what are they doing?"

"I don't know. I don't care, either."

I nodded, agreeing.

"Hey." He stopped, waiting for me to turn.

It wasn't until then that I got a good look at him. He'd cleaned up his boots and put on a clean shirt. I lifted my eyebrows when I saw that he'd even tucked it in.

"Look," he said, glancing at Ailee. "I'm sorry about last night."

"It's fine." The words came out curter than I meant them to. The words had been somewhat unforgivable, but even thinking about the feeling of his touch on my face again made me flush.

"No. It's not. I know you can handle yourself, but you don't always have to. You said yourself that we're partners, right?"

I looked into his eyes, trying to read him. "Yeah."

"That means that we need to trust each other."

"I know." I sighed.

That wasn't the problem. There was something about Koy that felt solid and steady to me. He was a knot that wouldn't easily break. In the last fourteen months, he'd proven that I could trust him, but if he had his brother watching me, then he didn't feel the same about me. I couldn't exactly blame him.

"From now on, I'll let you handle the Jevalis." I said.

He gave me a skeptical look.

"I mean it." I lifted my hands in the air. "I'll back off."

"Thank you."

"And I *can* handle myself."

A smirk broke on his lips. "I know you can."

Beside us, Ailee's lips were pressed together in a flat line. She was looking between us, waiting.

"You ready?" Koy said, eyes lifting to the other end of the harbor.

I exhaled. "Ready."

When bay twelve came into view, I picked up my pace, pressing through the crowd. A man and a woman were already waiting at the mouth of the slip, their fine jackets and shiny brass buckles noticeable on the dock of Narrows-born traders.

Koy waved to them as we approached and I reached to the

back of my belt. "Shit," I whispered, my steps slowing. "I forgot my ledger."

"No, you didn't." Ailee was beside me a second later, my ledger and a sharpened pencil pressed between her hands. She discreetly handed them to me before finding a place at my back to stand.

The man waiting at the bay greeted us with a nod, his white mustache combed and beard trimmed.

"This is Willa, our bosun." Koy gestured to me. "She'll be able to help you with whatever you need."

He looked me over carefully, brows coming together. The woman beside him didn't look convinced, either.

"How can I help?" I said, not breaking his gaze.

"Dennon." He finally reached out to shake my hand, an impressive gesture from a Saltblood. "I'm the *Wellworthy*'s helmsman. This is our navigator, Nathaly."

"Pleasure to meet you."

"We have some repairs in our second quarters we need done, but we're on a tight schedule."

"Understood."

The four of us looked at each other for a beat too long.

"If you show me, I can go ahead and get started." I offered.

Dennon nodded again, moving aside so that I could climb the ladder leading up to the deck. I stuck the ledger into back of my pants and climbed, and the thick smell of oiled wood grew heavy in the air. Even before I reached the deck, I could see that it was a pristine vessel. It couldn't be more than a few years old.

I came over the railing and Dennon followed as Koy and the coin master talked down on the dock. Ailee was waiting patiently beside them, not wanting to make a move until I told her to. At least one of us was good at listening.

I turned to the ship and several deckhands were at work on the masts, some of them restringing lines and others polishing the rust off of pulleys. None of them seemed concerned with me or the island, their attention on their work.

"This way."

Dennon led me toward the helm. It sat before the mouth of a wide, ornately carved archway beneath the upper decks. I smelled it before I saw it. Black char stained the wood just inside, the evidence of a fire.

I followed him into the passageway, inspecting the damage. The ruined wood paneling darkened as we neared one of the closed doors. That was where the fire must have broken out.

Dennon raised a fist, knocking twice, and I could feel the confusion twist my features. I'd never seen a helmsman knock on any door of his own ship. Had I heard him wrong? Had I gotten the two titles mixed up somehow?

Dennon gave me a taut but polite smile, as if his patience was being tried. When there was no sound inside the quarters, he knocked again.

A loud ping hit the floor on the other side of the door and I could feel the vibration of it under my feet. Something had fallen. It was followed by the scrape of wood and a couple of clumsy steps before the handle finally turned.

The door swung open and a young man stood on the other

side, leaning heavily into the jamb. His blond hair fell into his face, half of it tucked behind one ear as if he'd made no attempt at taming it. His shirt was crumpled, his boot laces untied, and despite a very handsome face, he was an utter mess.

His eyes slowly moved over my body before they met mine straight on in a level of eye contact that made me want to flinch. He'd clearly spent the night drinking. I could smell that, too.

"Sir, this is the harbor's bosun." Dennon clasped his hands behind his back. Was this man a helmsman or a butler? I couldn't tell. "She's here to take a look at the damage so she can make repairs."

The man, who couldn't be more than four or five years older than me, stared at me.

"Willa," I said, my own name sounding like a question. I had no idea what was going on here.

The young man stood up straighter, letting the door open wider. Behind him, the half-burned quarters were in complete disarray. There was a hole in the bulkhead between this room and the upper decks, where a patch of blue sky was visible.

"Coen Fuerst." He held out a hand and I reluctantly took it, shaking. His grip was tight and warm, matching that smolder in his gaze as he watched me.

"As you can see." Dennon stepped inside, going to the place on the wall that was the blackest. "The fire broke out here. Most of the damage is localized, thanks to the quick work of the crew, but we'll need to put it right before continuing on."

I studied the pattern of the burns. It looked like it had

originated beside the bed before it climbed the wall and spread across the floor. My guess was that Coen had knocked over a lantern in his drunken stupor. He was lucky he hadn't caught fire himself.

As if he could hear the thought, a wry smile lifted at the corner of his mouth. It made his eyes sparkle mischievously.

I pressed a hand to the wood panels, systematically leaning into each section to test its give. Most of the wall and floor looked as if they were sound, which meant the real work would be in repairing the ceiling. Everything else was a matter of sanding and re-staining. Those were tasks Ailee had mastered already, which meant I could get this done quickly and efficiently.

I took the ledger from my belt and started taking notes. "I have everything I need here on the island. Shouldn't take more than three days. Four, at most."

"Good." Dennon glanced at Coen and for the first time, I saw the hint of reproach in the helmsman. Whoever Coen was, this poor man clearly had the job of babysitting him. "Just let us know what you need. You can get started as soon as is convenient to you."

"Thank you."

I didn't miss the fact that he hadn't asked for a price, and I imagined it was because whatever I'd charge would be a drop in the bucket for a ship like this one. The bronze on the bowsprit alone would pay for it ten times over.

I closed the ledger, tucking it under my arm. "Anything else?"

"That should do it," Dennon answered.

Coen reached up, buttoning his shirt without taking his eyes off me. There was no mistaking the suggestive nature of that look. "Now." He raked one hand through his hair. "Where can I get a drink?"

FOUR

Koy was already waiting with a fresh pot of tea when I arrived at the tavern the next morning, his ledgers open before him.

"You missed quite a scene last night," Speck said, both hands in a bucket of suds. He was working his way through the stack of dirty glasses that lined the counter.

I looked around me at the empty tavern. The evidence of last night's chaos was still littered about the tables, the birds grazing along the docks for the crumbs left behind.

I grinned. "I take it things went well?"

"Very well." Speck flung the water from his hands, drying them on his apron. "Those Saltblood bastards spent triple the coin in one night that the Narrows-born crews do. Could get used to that."

"You might have to." I climbed onto the stool beside Koy, sliding his almost empty cup toward me. "So?" I filled it with tea, taking a sip.

He held up a hand, eyes still skipping over the numbers as

he finished the sums in his head. He had that look I recognized on his face—the one that said he was focused. From the beginning, he'd taken his job as harbor master more seriously than I'd expected, which was probably one of the reasons all of this had worked.

He made another mark with the quill before he set it down, taking the cup from my hands and drinking. "He's right. More than triple."

My smile widened and he handed the tea back to me.

"Another ship just arrived from Sowan, too. They've got a full hull so we can probably do some trading and get enough rye to last us until our order comes in. How's it going with the repairs?"

"Good. Got the unsalvageable wood torn out yesterday and the new planks should be cut and ready for me when I get down there. It's just a matter of getting everything replaced and sealed. I'm running low on tung oil, so Ailee's waiting for the merchant's house to open to get some more. Should be done in a couple of days."

"Might go faster if you hire a couple of hands to help you."

I glared at him. "Let me guess. The Jevalis aren't happy that I'm not recruiting workers for that ship."

"They are not," Speck chimed in, looking between us.

"Yeah, they left me a little present last night."

Koy turned to face me. "What do you mean?"

I shrugged. "There was a dead rat at the door of my post this morning."

Koy exhaled. "Who?"

"Does it matter? They all want to drag me down to that beach and drown me."

Koy didn't look amused. "I'll find out who did it and handle it."

"That's not what I meant when I agreed to let you deal with them," I said, giving him a meaningful look. "Crews do it on ships all the time. They're harmless."

Koy didn't look convinced.

"They're not too keen about the Saltbloods drinking all the rye, either," Speck added.

"If it means copper in our pockets, the crew of the *Wellworthy* can have every last bottle of rye on this island. And I'm not changing my mind. Bruin and his guys aren't stepping foot on that brig."

Koy ran a hand over the back of his head, letting his ledger fall closed. He knew I was right. He had to. The bigger problem would come if I actually got what I wanted out of this deal. If more ships from the Unnamed Sea started showing up at our docks, I wouldn't be able to control who worked on what ship. At some point, it would become like every other harbor in the Narrows, theft and rotten deals included. I just needed to keep it at bay long enough to get more ships in the harbor.

"What about this Coen guy?" I changed the subject, looking to Speck.

His eyes drifted to one of the shanties turned inn rooms at the end of the nearest dock. "He spent a few hours in here looking for someone to take to bed before he disappeared. Haven't seen him since."

I rolled my eyes, unsurprised.

"Took a whole bottle of rye with him."

"As long as he paid for it," I muttered.

"Oh, he paid for it." Speck laughed. "About twice over. Not sure he was even looking at how much copper he was laying down."

I turned back to Koy. "You find anything out about this guy?"

Koy checked over his shoulder before he answered. "He's the son of some big merchant in Bastian. The navigator made it sound like he's fallen out of his father's good graces and somehow, they got landed with him."

That explained the strange interaction between Coen and Dennon yesterday. Dennon was the helmsman of the *Wellworthy*, but Coen's father probably held a contract on the ship.

"Where are they headed next?"

"Dern. Ceros after that, then Sowan."

"What are they doing at all these ports?"

Koy shrugged. "Maybe mapping out a new trade route, setting up new contracts? There are more and more of them every month."

"All the more reason to make sure Jeval is on the map."

Koy nodded.

"Just make sure they enjoy the rest of their stay, Speck. Even if you need to dip into the emergency stores of rye."

"Understood." He nodded, hands on his hips.

He was enjoying this. We all were. For the last year, Koy

and I had done nothing but build this place from the ground up, plank by plank. We'd torn out the old docks, reconstructed and expanded them, given loans to the island's makers to build up inventories of supplies, and even helped fund Speck's tavern. Now, it was all very close to paying off.

I drained the teacup and refilled it, sliding it back in front of Koy. "You know, I think we just might pull this off."

He smiled, and this wasn't the wry, mocking grin that usually adorned his face. This was his real smile, something I'd only seen a few times before. "I think you might be right."

I slid off the stool just as the door to the inn room creaked open and all three of us looked up. Coen was coming up the dock, disheveled blond hair blowing in the wind and shirt half-untucked. He squinted as if the sunlight hurt his eyes, but when he spotted us, his suave, cool expression returned.

"Morning." He made his way toward us.

"Good morning." I nodded.

He was, somehow, incredibly handsome despite the rye-soaked look on his face. Saltbloods, especially ones from Bastian, seemed to have an inexplicable ability to appear polished no matter the circumstances.

Coen gave Speck a nod, gesturing to the teapot, and Speck obediently turned on his heel, heading to the kettle suspended over the coals.

"This is Koy, our harbor master," I said.

Coen gave his hand a shake. "Pleased to meet you."

"Likewise," Koy answered.

"And how are things going in my ill-fated quarters?"

Coen returned his attention to me and I realized he was closer than I found comfortable. Beside me, Koy seemed to notice, too. His eyes dropped to my shoulder, where Coen's sleeve brushed mine before I took a discreet step backward. There was a lack of distance about Coen that I didn't like, but I imagined there were plenty of people at each port who found it charming.

"We're making headway," I said, "it'll be good as new in two or three days."

"Wonderful."

"I hope it's not too much of an inconvenience. I know you have to be on your way."

Coen laughed. "I have exactly nowhere to be. Take your time."

I studied him, thinking it was an odd thing to say.

"I know poor Dennon likes to keep a schedule, but he'll manage."

Poor Dennon. There was that condescension again. I imagined it was difficult for the helmsman to resist the urge to smack Coen on a daily basis.

Speck set down another teapot. He'd chosen one without chips or cracks in it, and I met his eyes for a silent beat in appreciation.

"Why don't you let me buy you two a drink tonight? A thank-you for your impeccable hospitality."

"That's not necess—" Koy started, but I cut him off.

"That's very kind, thank you."

Coen shot a look at Koy, clearly amused by the exchange.

"Good." He pulled the pocket watch from his vest. "Should we say about seven?"

"Sure," Koy managed.

The door to Coen's inn room squeaked again and when I saw who came out, I had to bite my bottom lip to keep my mouth from falling open. It was Raef. He looked like he'd just rolled out of bed, his shirt off and draped over one shoulder. The muscles in his sculpted arms flexed under the skin as he tied his hair back in a knot at the nape of his neck.

I immediately looked to Koy, who was watching his brother saunter up the dock, headed for the main harbor.

Koy's gaze slid back to Speck, his annoyance only barely at bay. He'd failed to mention who Coen had eventually found to take to bed with him last night.

"Well, I'd better get started," I said, breaking the tension. "Ailee will be waiting for me."

"I'll walk with you," Koy said.

Coen took a seat at the counter and we walked shoulder to shoulder toward the main dock that led around the barrier islands to the harbor. Raef was already out of sight.

"I don't like that guy," Koy muttered.

"Really?" I laughed. "I couldn't tell."

"What the hell is Raef thinking? The crews from the Narrows are one thing, but . . ." He shook his head. "All we need is a jealous Saltblood on our hands."

"I hardly think Coen will be jealous of anything. I'm pretty sure he was inviting *me* to bed when I met him yesterday."

Koy stopped walking, forcing me to turn back. He leveled his gaze at me.

"What?" I was laughing again.

"What do you mean *he was inviting you to bed*?"

"Not actually inviting me. But there were definitely some insinuations. You know men like that."

I waited for him to say something, but he was quiet.

"Koy?"

"If you want me to behave around that bastard, I need you to not spend the night in his room."

I gaped at him. *"What?"*

"I'm serious."

"So am I," I snapped. "Why would you even say that?"

"I just feel like I need to be really clear about what will happen."

"I don't know if you've noticed, Koy, but I don't exactly make a habit out of climbing into bed with crew."

"He's not crew."

I groaned. "You know what I mean."

"And *you* know what *I* mean," he said, letting the weight of the words settle.

I didn't want to admit it, even to myself. Koy and I had an unspoken understanding and so far, it had worked. We didn't call attention to or acknowledge the fact that there was a very real, very dangerous tether forming between us. It had started the first day he stepped foot on the *Marigold*, and it had followed us here, to Jeval. We were partners, but we were also more than that, and this was the first time he was calling it out.

"You don't want me to break that guy's face? Then don't let me find out that you're messing around with him."

I exhaled. "I'm not."

"Good."

He looked at me another moment before he finally started walking, shouldering around me to head up the dock. I waited until he disappeared before I followed.

‹▾›

FIVE

‹▴›

"Alright, let's hear it," I said.

Ailee lowered down to her haunches in the middle of Coen's dimly lit quarters, looking over the tools I'd laid out on the floor. She'd mastered the names and uses of the different nogs, nails, and larger tools, but so far, she'd failed to get the irons right.

Her black, curly hair was barely contained in the scarf wrapped around her head, the frayed ends of the cloth dangling from a knot at the nape of her neck. Her hand hovered over the first iron, the name still coming to her. It was the one she usually missed. "Meaking iron." She looked up to me for confirmation before she pointed to the next, then the next, "Sail iron, horsing iron . . ." She bit her lip, thinking about the last one. "Reeming iron?"

I grinned. "That's right. So, which do you need?"

"The meaking iron," she answered.

I nodded. "Well done."

She picked it up, smiling wide as she went to the exposed

timbers of the dismantled wall that was waiting to be reframed. She'd use the iron to scrape the old oakum from where it had once stuffed the spaces between the planks. I'd be right behind her, replacing them so that when she was finished, she could fill the cracks with new oakum.

"When do I get to go up in the masts?" she asked, glancing at me over her shoulder.

"When you learn to use the harness correctly."

"I can't learn if you won't teach me."

"There's about a hundred other things you need to master before you go climbing up in the lines like a stowaway rat," I said.

Even from here, I could tell she was pursing her lips. But unlike me, Ailee knew when to hold her tongue and how to be patient. From day one as my apprentice, all she'd wanted to do was climb the masts, and her light weight and small frame would make it easy for her. But I remembered clearly the first time I'd fallen from the ropes, nearly killing myself when I was her age.

I took up the next wooden plank, feeling along its edge to be sure it was straight. It wasn't easy to get raw oak on the island and Koy had questioned the expense, but having the stores had paid off now that we had a ship like the *Wellworthy* to repair.

"How many nogs per plank?" I asked, testing her again.

She arched an eyebrow at me. "Per plank, or per *end* of plank?"

I couldn't hold back my smile now. "Per end."

"Three."

"Correct."

We worked side by side, her clearing the oakum and me laying the new planks until the wall that had once been a blackened, fire-eaten mess was reconstructed. The new wood was pale compared to the older oak, and if Coen could keep from setting it aflame again, it would last a dozen years or more. My eyes roamed over the bulkhead, where the carved edges caught the light. It made sense that Coen was the son of a gem merchant. No detail had gone overlooked, no adornment spared in these quarters. Ships like this one lasted generations, its helmsman's honor and prestige reflected in its elegance. But if the *Wellworthy* wasn't trading gems and jewelry, what was it doing in the Narrows?

Ailee packed up the tools as I took the rectangle of sandstone to the walls, wiping back and forth until it was free of any straggling splinters. The last step would be to oil the wood, which would take two consecutive days. We wouldn't be able to match the color, but at least Coen would have a roof over his head again, and then the *Wellworthy* would be on its way.

It was nearly dark by the time Ailee and I were climbing down the ladder to the docks. She was tired, like every other night, her eleven-year-old body struggling to keep up with the backbreaking work of being a bosun. I remembered that feeling. I also remember wanting the job bad enough to do it anyway.

When she started in the opposite direction of the tavern, I stopped her. "Supper, Ailee."

"Do I have to?"

I took the heavy tool belt from her shoulder and she stretched her arm, now free of its weight. "There's no more porridge at the post. Come on."

Reluctantly, she followed me up the dock. The island was cast in a dark pink glow, the somewhat calm water reflecting the last of the light. One of the young men Speck paid to clean up after his patrons was on the floor of the tavern when we arrived, wiping up a smear of blood. There were three chairs toppled over, but whatever had taken place, it was over now.

I spotted Coen and Koy at a table along the edge of the dock before I handed Ailee two coppers for a bowl of stew and a small loaf of bread. Then she pressed herself between the tables, headed for the man who was standing over a large, steaming pot.

Most of the Jevalis liked Ailee better than they liked me, but that wasn't saying much. The man barely looked at her as he took her coin, ladling the broth into the bowl without much care and tossing the smallest loaf into it. Ailee stared at the sopping mess before she picked it up, sipping from the lip. She didn't seem to mind.

I left her at the counter and Coen combed his neat blond hair back from his face with his hand as I took the seat in front of him. He'd managed to clean up and now he looked like a proper Saltblood, but there was still that haze of drink in his eyes.

"Dennon says the repairs are coming along. My quarters are at least whole again." He smirked.

144

"All patched up. We just have the sealing to do," I answered.

He nodded. "Impressive. I wasn't sure you'd get it done that quickly without a crew."

The comment sounded innocent enough, but there was a look in Coen's eye that said it held more meaning. Was he curious why I was working alone or annoyed because it could have gotten done quicker? I wasn't going to tell him I could trust the Jevalis as far as I could throw them, and I wasn't going to play down the job I'd done, either. So, instead of answering, I took a sip of my rye.

He did the same, hiding the smile on his lips. If we were sharing some kind of secret, I didn't know what it was.

A loud group of men came into the tavern, settling at the table behind us. It was the crew from the *Iris* and from the look of them, they'd already been drinking. That was the thing about crews. They didn't belong on land. Any stop that lasted more than a day or two was asking for trouble.

As soon as they sat, Speck was making his way toward them, glasses in hand.

"I hope Speck has been taking care of you?" Koy said, mustering his best harbor master tone.

I was relieved. I'd spent the day unsure if he'd be able to put aside the irritation he'd had about Coen last night, but now he was ready to do his job.

"He has," Coen answered. "Hopefully we'll be out of your way soon. I know the crew is probably drinking the island dry."

That was rich, coming from him. I was pretty sure that Coen had had his fair share of rye.

"Well, you're welcome back next time you're crossing to or from the Unnamed Sea. We'll be resupplied in a matter of days and we have plans for a drydock before next year."

I could feel Koy's reaction without even looking at him.

Coen's eyebrows lifted. "A drydock. Really?"

"That's right."

"Well, that is certainly something to keep in mind. Though, if you get a drydock you might not be able to handle all the ships that'll show up in that harbor."

I finally looked to Koy, not bothering to smooth over my smug expression.

He looked more annoyed than ever now. "So, you're headed to Sowan next?" He changed the subject.

"That's right."

"Is the *Wellworthy* setting up a trade route, or . . . ?"

"Not exactly."

"Something secret, then?" Koy pressed.

The men behind us began to sing a sloppy tavern song and I nudged Koy's knee with mine. The edge was coming back into his voice and if Coen hadn't already noticed, he would.

"Nothing that exciting, I'm afraid." Coen propped himself up on his elbows, folding his hands in front of his chin. "I've been tasked with righting my wrongs. I lost something of my father's, and now I'm expected to get it back."

"What is it? Maybe we can help," I said, watching Speck

make his way again to the rambunctious table behind us. This time, he had two bottles of rye raised in the air. The men started clapping when they saw him.

"It's not jewels or a ship or anything like that. It's a person. Two people, actually."

I leaned in closer, unsure if I'd heard him right through the singing voices at my back. "People?"

Coen met my eyes. "A silversmith. A man about my age with black hair and scars that cover his hands and arms. He's with a girl."

There was a chill in the air suddenly. I made a point of knowing who dropped anchor on these docks, and I hadn't seen anyone like that come through Jeval. But if he was talking about someone whose own soul was a debt, the way West's had been with Saint, then he wouldn't find any help from me. Or Koy. We didn't get involved in the business of traders.

When we said nothing, Coen laughed. "Yeah, I didn't think they would have come through here. But worth a try."

It was only then I noticed that Koy hadn't touched his rye. He still sat unmoving, his scrutinizing gaze roaming over Coen as if he was searching for something there.

"I've been banished from Bastian until I find them, and that's not looking like a feasible task. So, who knows, you might be seeing more of me." Coen winked.

"You're just going to float port to port?" I asked.

Coen shrugged. "Why not?"

That was a good question. Coen had his own personal envoy taking him around the Narrows and beyond so that he could drink and find brief companionship in tavern inns under the guise of making things right with his father. If I had to guess, I'd say he wasn't looking all that hard for the people he was supposed to find.

"She's got what she deserved, I'll tell you that much!" a man from the other table shouted, bring the song to a stop.

I turned to see one of the *Iris*'s new deckhands staring into his empty glass. The others went on with their conversation, but I couldn't take my eyes from him as he mumbled on.

"She thought I didn't see, but that handkerchief she carries is stained with blood." The man beside him blinked sleepily, clearly too drunk to even hear what the deckhand was saying. "No, the great Emilia Marley isn't long for this world. Mark my words. She'll be rotting by the end of next month."

I froze, hand tightening on my glass as I stared at the floor. A chill crept over me, a trail of pinpricks dotting my skin.

Emilia Marley was a crofter. Not just any crofter—*the* rye crofter in Sowan. The head of the rye guild and the mastermind behind the trade that had built an entire economy for the Narrows.

I tried to think. The *Iris* had just come from Sowan. Did this man know Emilia? And what exactly was he saying? That she was . . . *dying*?

I shifted in my seat, trying to listen. But if the man was still talking, it was drowned out by another song that had struck up among the crew.

My eyes shifted to Koy, who had finally lifted his glass to his mouth. By all appearances, he hadn't heard what I had.

But when I looked across the table to Coen, he was rigid, his gaze pinned on the table behind me.

Had he heard the name?

It wasn't the kind of harmless rumor that made its way through the taverns of the Narrows. This was something else. If what the man was saying was true, it had enormous consequences. Emilia had built an entire industry on the production of rye, giving the Narrows legs to stand on against the trade of the Unnamed Sea. She had also committed the lion's share of her inventory to one contract—Saint.

The less than equitable business relationship was a constant point of contention among rye merchants and even the Trade Council at large. But Emilia was the lynchpin. At the end of the day, she was a merchant, and merchants had control over their own contracts. There were only two ways to end one. The first was for the merchant to dissolve it themselves.

The second was for the merchant to . . . die.

As soon as I thought it, Coen relaxed back into his chair, the calm demeanor returning to his face. Had I imagined his reaction? He was sitting farther away than Koy was. It was possible he hadn't heard anything at all.

"Yeah, I'm not in any hurry," he said, returning his attention to Koy.

I'd forgotten what we were talking about, my heart still racing.

I looked around me at the tavern filled to the brim with Saltbloods. The words the man had uttered weren't just a scrap of news. They were a vulnerability. A secret that, in the right hands, could compromise the Narrows.

"I'd better get going," I said, getting to my feet.

Koy's brow cinched as he looked up at me. Coen, too, looked surprised by the abruptness of my exit.

"I've got supplies to prep for tomorrow and Ailee will be waiting," I lied.

Koy looked suspicious, but Coen was already refilling his glass of rye. "Good night then."

I forced a tight smile and kept my pace slow as I headed for the harbor. The rumble of the open-air tavern was replaced by the soft slosh of water beneath the docks.

I'd met Emilia before, because Saint had had the *Marigold* making deliveries to her on a schedule. We'd been at her croft at least once a month until we got all but banished from Sowan. As soon as it got out that West had set that fire in Lander's warehouse, we'd been prevented from docking and as far as I knew, the *Marigold* still wasn't welcome there. But if there was any truth to what the man from the *Iris* had said, any at all, then I needed to be sure the information got to the right people first.

I slipped into my post, closing the door behind me. Moonlight streamed through the open window where Ailee's hammock was strung up over the floor. I lit the lantern, searching for my ink pot.

I didn't like the idea of sending such sensitive information in a letter, but I wouldn't be able to leave Jeval myself for at least two days. By then, anything could happen.

W—I scribbled across the parchment. *News came through Jeval today you should look into. If you can get to Sowan and check on our old drop there, you should. As soon as possible.*

That was as clear as I was willing to get in a message that would pass through multiple hands. I sealed the parchment and addressed it to the Port of Ceros, where it would be waiting for West when he got in from Dern. If the letter left on the *Featherback* tomorrow, it would beat the *Marigold* there.

SIX

I paced the dock at a clip, sending a huddled flock of seabirds flying.

The letter burned in my vest pocket as my eyes scanned the ships in the harbor. Most of the crews were just beginning to wake, their duties trimmed as long as they were anchored, but the *Featherback* was bustling, the deckhands up in the masts and getting ready to set sail.

I glanced over my shoulder to the harbor master's post. The shutters of the single window were still closed, which meant that if Koy was up, he wasn't open for business yet.

Fret was already set up in his chair when I made it to the end of the docks, his collection of strange wares on display at his feet. I pulled the copper from my pocket before I'd even reached him.

"Morning." He looked up at me warily, gray eyes flat against the brilliant blue sea.

I found a place to lean on the railing, more closely than usual. "Hey, Fret."

Two men came down the ladder of the nearest ship, headed for the merchant's house. I watched them, waiting until they were out of earshot.

"Everything okay?" Fret's brow wrinkled with concern.

"Yeah," I forced a smile. "Just checking in to see if you've heard anything."

He tucked the copper into his jacket. "Just the usual. Bruin grumbling to whoever will listen, some dredgers from the beach complaining about the trades yesterday."

"Is that it?"

Fret crossed his arms, leaning back in his rickety chair. He was suspicious now. "Something in particular you're after?"

I lowered my voice. "Nothing new going around since that ship the *Iris* came in? Rumors or anything?"

His bottom lip jutted out as he thought about it. "No, don't think so."

I exhaled, relieved. "Okay. Thanks."

"No problem, Willa."

I started back the way I'd come, gaze fixed on the *Featherback* in the distance. It was usual practice to send messages to other ports through the helmsmen of ships, and they were bound by agreements with the Trade Council to treat them with discretion. But that didn't mean that I trusted them to get my letter to West all the way to Ceros unread. If someone did open my letter, they wouldn't find anything damning, but it was enough to peak curiosity and that made me nervous.

The bigger problem was that I was almost sure Koy wouldn't approve of my sending it. We'd agreed from the beginning that we wouldn't get involved in the business of traders, and I'd already broken that promise once when I bought Ailee from her helmsman. Koy hadn't let me forget it, either.

I stopped walking when I saw that the harbor master's post window was now open. I could walk straight past it and give my message to the *Featherback* and Koy would know no different. Eventually, however, if what the deckhand said last night was true and this thing blew up the way I thought it would, it might come out that the news originated here on Jeval. And Koy wasn't stupid. It wouldn't take long for him to put together what I'd done.

What happened with Ailee had been different. I knew that. I'd given her the protection no one else would because I knew what it was like to *be* her. But I'd paid fairly, taken her room and board on myself, and we'd kept business with the ship she'd been on. We were no worse for wear, even if I had less coin to show for it.

This letter in my pocket—that felt like a lie.

I pulled the watch from my pocket and checked the time. If I was going to get the first coat of seal done on the *Wellworthy* before sundown, I needed to get started, but there was no getting around the fact that if Koy and I were partners—and we were—then I owed him the truth. If we couldn't trust each other, we wouldn't last another year in this harbor.

I knocked on the door of his post, almost instantly regretting it. Through the window, I could see him slipping his faded white shirt over his head, the sliding over dark, tanned skin. His trousers hung low on his hips, and since he'd shaved his long hair off, his shoulders looked even broader over his narrow waist.

There were times when I let myself look at him. There were even times when I imagined myself touching him, but there was a self-imposed limit to how much I'd let myself feel. The clear boundary I never crossed was the moment that warm liquid feeling surfaced in the center of my chest. That's the place I kept my toes on the sand. Just far enough from the break of the wave to not be pulled out to sea.

When he opened the door, he looked surprised to see me. "Oh, Willa." He didn't have that sleepy look, so he'd likely been up for a while, going over his manifests.

"Morning," I said, gesturing inside. "Can I come in?"

"Sure." He let me pass, closing the door behind me.

The post wasn't much bigger than mine, built to be both his home and his office. From the window, he could see the full length of the harbor from the first bay to the last. Only a year ago we'd stood on the old, crumbling docks together planning the exact spot for this place. It still smelled like freshly planed wood.

"I need to talk to you about something," I said.

Koy stoppered the ink pot on his little table, but I could tell he was already listening.

"Last night, I heard something in the tavern. Something . . . important."

"All right." He waited.

I swallowed. "Do you know who Emilia Marley is?"

"The rye crofter?"

I nodded. "She's also the rye guild's master."

"Yeah, I know who she is."

"When we were having a drink with Coen, I heard someone from the *Iris* say something." I hesitated.

"Spit it out, Willa." Koy almost laughed.

"It sounded like she's sick. Like maybe she's dying."

The smile melted from Koy's face.

"And, I don't know, the way he said it was almost as if it was being kept secret."

"Well, if it's true, then I'm sure they aren't advertising it. I mean, if Emilia Marley died, that would . . ." He tried to find the words.

"Change everything," I finished.

He met my eyes in a silent agreement.

"If Emilia dies and her contracts die with her, every merchant and trader in the Narrows will be tearing each other apart for a seat at that table. And it won't just affect them. The guild, the Trade Council, it would disrupt every facet of our trade, our ports, our copper, everything."

"We don't know that she isn't making arrangements."

"Maybe she is. Maybe she isn't."

"We don't even know if it's true, Willa." His voice rose. "You're putting a lot of stock into a rumor you heard at a tavern from a drunk deckhand."

He was right. But I couldn't shake the feeling I'd had last night, like I was holding my breath. Like I was carrying a secret that wasn't mine.

"I think we should tell West. Just let him know that—"

"No," Koy answered, cutting me off. "No way."

"Why not?"

"Because that is the exact opposite of staying impartial in trade business. You can't just tip off the *Marigold* every time we have valuable information."

"That's not what I mean. I just think we should let him know," I pressed. "Just in case. He could go there, make sure that nothing's going on."

"It's none of our business."

"How can you say that?" I gaped at him. "If this is true, it could affect *all* of us."

"Traders and merchants rise and fall. That's how things go. This is no different."

"It is and you know it," I said. "Imagine if someone from the Unnamed Sea found out before our own Trade Council. We can't just keep this to ourselves."

"Yes, we can. And that's what we're going to do."

"Koy."

"How are we supposed to run like a real port if we're passing on rumors from trading ships and getting mixed up in their affairs? There's supposed to be a separation between us and them. You know that."

"I also know that's not how ports really work. They break those rules all the time."

"It's how *we* work. How we *agreed* to work. Those ports have the luxury of ships needing them. They have villages and cities and resources. We haven't earned the right to break the rules yet. This is the first of many times we'll be in this position. We'll have ships from the Narrows and the Unnamed Sea docked side by side every single day. You think we won't hear things?"

I rubbed my hands over my face, trying to think.

"You keeping saying you want to make your own way, Willa? Then do it."

I glared at him. "That is what I'm doing. I'm here. I left everything, gave all of my copper to be here."

"And now you want to run to West the moment you feel like you need to."

"That's not what I'm doing! I'm not running to anyone!" I was shouting now, and I didn't care who out on the docks could hear me.

"Have you broken from him or not?"

I stared at him. *Broken* wasn't the right word. I'd never be broken from my brother. But the real question Koy was asking me was what I was choosing. West and the *Marigold* and my life before, or Jeval and the port and my new life here. With him.

"I have." I breathed. "You know I have."

"Then you know you can't send a message to West."

I grit my teeth, eyes pinned to the floor as heat licked my face. Koy was the only one seeing this clearly. It wasn't clean or simple, but the bottom line was that there were consequences we could both face if I inserted myself into an unfolding crisis of this magnitude. We had to be impartial. And Koy wasn't wrong about the fact that it could all be a lie. I could be making all of this into something it wasn't.

"All right," I said. "You're right."

Koy's eyebrows lifted. "I'm sorry?"

"I said, you're right."

A smile broke on his face. "I don't know if you've ever said that before."

"Very funny," I muttered. "I have to go. I'm running behind as it is."

I opened the door and stepped back out into the sunlight, closing it behind me. When I looked back, Koy was watching me from the window as he picked up the quill on his table. He still had that smug look, but the teasing in his eyes made my heart flutter just a little bit.

Ailee was waiting for me at the mouth of the slip where the *Wellworthy* was anchored in the distance. Her black curls were flying in a cloud around her head, her attention on something across the docks. It wasn't until I got closer that I could make out the expression on her face. She was worried about something. Maybe even scared.

I picked up my pace, opening my mouth to call out to her when I heard voices shouting. When I passed the next ship, I could finally see what she was looking at. A crowd was gathered a few bays down, lining the edge of one of the docks where it followed the black rock face. They were peering down into the water.

"Get a hook!" someone called out, and a woman went running.

More people were appearing on the decks of the ships, streaming toward the bows to see what was going on. I pushed through the crowd when I reached them, prying a path between the bodies until I reached the edge.

I froze when I caught sight of what they were looking at, my hand flying to my mouth. It was a body. Floating face down in the water.

There was no rescue being made because it was clear the person was dead. A few crabs had already been eating at the man and he was drained of color in a way that only happened after many hours in the water.

The woman reappeared with a large iron hook in hand and someone fished the man from the sea. The throng of people moved back as they pulled him up onto the dock and as soon as he rolled over, face to the sun, all the air left my lungs.

It was him. The man from the *Iris* I'd seen last night. The one who'd been talking about Emilia.

It was bound to happen eventually, but in the year we'd been operating, we'd never had a death of a visiting crew occur. It just so happened that it was now, and it had happened to a man who'd been slurring dangerous rumors at the tavern. That couldn't be a coincidence.

My eyes roamed the faces that surrounded me, looking for anyone who didn't look shocked by the sight. If I'd heard him, it was completely possible that others had, too. But I hadn't seen a single reaction last night, not even from the numb-faced man who sat beside the deckhand. The only moment I thought I'd caught a glimpse of something was when I'd turned back around and seen that almost imperceptible rigidness in Coen.

I lifted my gaze to the *Wellworthy* in the distance, my blood running cold.

There, on the deck, he was leaning into the foremast, hands stuffed in the pockets of his unbuttoned jacket. But when he caught my eyes on him, he turned into the wind, disappearing.

SEVEN

All but a single sliver of light was shut out of the helmsman's quarters as the door closed, the window fastened tight. The helmsman of the *Iris* stood before his desk in the glow of a lantern, arms crossed over his chest as his gaze moved from me to Koy.

The ship was one that had visited before and we'd managed to work out an agreement for supplies to be couriered from Ceros once a month, but this could wreck everything.

"Did he have any disagreements with the crew that you're aware of?" Koy asked, playing the part of harbor watch. We didn't have one of those, something that I now realized had been a mistake.

"Hasn't been around long enough to make any enemies. We just hired him on in Sowan. He was working there on a croft for a few years, didn't seem to know anyone when he came on board."

That lined up, if the deckhand had really known Emilia.

If he had worked on a croft in Sowan, there was every reason to believe it was hers.

"None of the crew seems to know where he went last night, so that's no help." He added.

"Look, I think the most likely scenario here is that this was an accident," Koy said.

I turned toward him just slightly, trying not to give away what I was thinking. Koy knew as well as I did that the odds of this man being the one to say what he had about Emilia *and* ending up dead the same night were slim.

"We were both at the tavern last night and we saw him. He'd definitely had more than a few drinks, and I think your crew would say the same."

"With these barrier islands," I added, "it can be dangerous if you fall in. Especially in the dark."

The helmsman seemed to buy it. "Just as reasonable as any other explanation."

"If you'd like, we can take care of the body," Koy said.

I shivered. It wasn't the first dead man I'd seen. Far from it, in fact. But the significance of the timing made a chill creep over my skin. I could feel it. Something about all of this wasn't right.

"I'd appreciate it."

"And we'd appreciate your discretion." Koy's voice deepened with meaning.

"As far as I'm concerned, you two have done right by the *Iris*. No reason to muck that up now. But this happens again, and we'll be having a different conversation."

I nodded in agreement. We were responsible for what

happened in our harbor just like he was responsible for what happened on his ship. If it got around that crews were disappearing on our docks and washing up on the beach, that would be a problem. One that could sink us before we even really got our legs beneath us.

"If there's nothing else, I do need to get the ship underway."

"Of course." Koy gave the helmsman a grateful nod and the door opened again, flooding the cabin with bright light.

We didn't speak as we crossed the deck and climbed down the ladder. We didn't so much as look at each other until we'd reached the main dock, the *Iris* out of sight.

"What the hell is this?" Koy muttered through clenched teeth.

"How long did you stay with Coen last night?"

"What?"

I stopped, turning toward him.

"When you left last night," I whispered, "did you see where he went? Did he go back to his room or to the harbor?"

Koy was trying to follow my thinking, but he was coming up short. "I have no idea. What does it matter?"

"I think." I paused, weighing the cost of what I was about to say. "I'm pretty sure he heard the same thing I did last night."

He stared at me.

"When I looked back at him after the deckhand said what he said, he had this expression like he was as shocked to hear it as I was. But then he smoothed it over, like he hadn't heard, and I thought I'd imagined it."

"Maybe you did."

A woman with a string of fish passed, eyeing us as we fell quiet. I waited until she'd reached the next bay before I continued.

"If you didn't see where he went last night, he could've have followed that man."

"But why kill him?"

I shrugged. "I don't know. To make sure he doesn't repeat what he said?"

Koy wasn't buying it. "You think the deckhand was murdered by that tidy merchant's son?" Koy laughed. "I doubt he can even throw a punch, Willa."

I shook my head. He was wrong about that. I didn't know how I knew, but I did. There was an edge to Coen beneath his charm. A coldness brimming beneath that look in his eye.

"Just . . . just tell Raef to stay away from him. I mean it, Koy."

Koy looked at me for a long moment before his eyes went over my head. "Great. What now?"

Down the dock, the helmsman of a schooner called the *Grouse* was stalking toward us, three of his crew on his heels. Even from here, I could tell he was furious.

I positioned myself next to Koy and when the helmsman reached us, he tossed a coin purse to the dock. Its contents spilled out, falling through the cracks. It was nothing more than what looked to be lead pellets.

My gaze lifted to meet his.

"This is the third time in two days I've found a swapped purse. Third time!" he shouted.

Koy lifted a hand in the air that was meant to calm the

man, but it only made him draw a knife. I stepped forward, my hand going to the handle of my dagger. Before I could pull it, Koy grabbed me, holding me in place.

"I want three full purses by sundown. Then we're raising anchor and we're not coming back." He seethed.

Koy kept his tone even. "I apologize for the—"

"We came here to do business, not lose coin."

"I know. And believe me, we will find whoever is responsible and we'll make it right."

The man lowered his knife and shoved between us, starting toward the tavern. "Sundown!" he called back over his shoulder, slipping his blade into his belt.

I rounded on Koy, my hands clenched into fists. "You'll handle them, huh?" I said, daring him to argue.

I didn't give him a chance to respond, starting toward the other end of the harbor where I knew Bruin and his friends would be waiting to catch a skiff back to the beach.

"Willa."

Koy's voice was barely audible over my racing thoughts. I'd known this would happen. I'd known the minute I stepped foot on this island and Bruin fixed me with that demeaning look that he was going to be trouble. That he'd cost us if we didn't deal with him.

My boots pounded on the dock and the closer I got, the higher the scream was rising in my throat. Bruin didn't see me coming until I was shoving him in the chest with both hands, nearly knocking him into the water.

"What the—"

Koy caught up to me just in time to put himself between me and Bruin.

"Your pickpocketing just cost us a ship," I spat. "You're going to pay every single coin back. *Now*."

Bruin laughed and the others joined, making my head swim. He didn't get it. None of them did. They didn't understand what we were trying to do here or what this place meant. They never would.

For the first time since I'd come to Jeval, I felt so utterly foolish for being here. For thinking that this idea, this dream could be real. I'd spent almost every coin I had on this harbor and left everything I'd known. And for what?

"You need to get your *girl* under control, Koy."

I reared back and swung my fist as hard as I could, knuckles slamming into Bruin's cheek. Pain exploded between every bone in my hand, making me gasp, and I cradled it against my chest.

As soon as he got his balance, Bruin was lunging for me. Koy caught him by the shirt with both hands, driving him back until he hit the post behind him. He pinned Bruin there, peering down into his face with a look I hadn't seen before.

Everyone on the dock went quiet as he began to speak. "You just lost your permit to trade in this harbor," he said, voice like thunder.

Bruin's eyes lit with panic. "Permit? What permit?"

"The one I'm issuing today to every Jevali who wants the right to trade on *our* docks."

"You can't do that!"

"Yes." Koy shoved into him once more before letting him go. "I can. You risk our business and you risk the future of every Jevali on this island. If you don't see that, you don't belong here."

Shock riddled every face that surrounded us, including mine. I'd never seen him like this with a Jevali. My guess was that no one had.

"You pay back the coin, take a skiff to the beach, and if I see you back here or in the merchant's house again, you *will* regret it." He turned to the others. "Anyone else?"

A few heads shook nervously. No one spoke up.

It was only then that I noticed the skiff full of dredgers behind us. It had pulled up in the chaos of what had just unfolded, and every one of them had seen the exchange between me, Koy, and Bruin.

"Well?" Koy flung a hand toward the spectators in the harbor. "You have work to do, or what?"

They dredgers climbed out of the skiff one by one until it was empty and Bruin stepped inside, making it rock. There was a scratch on his cheek where I'd hit him and the bloom of red below his cheekbone was spreading. Between my fingers, the pain was only growing. I was pretty sure I'd broken something.

The woman running the skiff avoided Koy's gaze, turning the small sail before she pushed off from the dock. Bruin's eyes didn't leave mine as it caught the wind, drifting toward the beach.

Koy sighed, watching the boat grow smaller in the distance. "We're going to pay for that."

EIGHT

The thick scent of tung oil burned in my nose as I watched a single star move across the sky. The breeze coming through the window wasn't strong enough to cool the cramped bosun's post, but it carried the smell of a storm—a scent that made me miss the *Marigold*.

I'd never felt that way about the hovel we called home in Waterside. I didn't miss the streets that always seemed to be wet, even if it hadn't rained, or the sounds of the city. I didn't miss my mother, either.

I just missed West.

The *Marigold* was the first place I ever had to come back to. A place that I belonged. And now that I was gone, I couldn't quite remember why I'd been so set on leaving. For the last few hours, as I painted oil onto the unsealed wood in Coen's quarters, I'd been asking myself the same questions over and over.

Had I made a mistake when I came here? Was any of this even real? Could I really make it without my brother?

I could see it in my mind, everything falling apart piece

by piece. The harbor, the port, all the copper I'd sunk into this dream. It was all crumbling before my very eyes. How had I been so stupid?

Only a few steps away, Ailee's soft breaths echoed the faint brush of waves outside. She was curled up in her hammock, one foot dangling from the fabric. We'd worked until well after sundown to finish the sealing in Coen's quarters and after another coat, the *Wellworthy* would be on its way. Their departure couldn't come soon enough, and while only days ago I'd been convinced it was our big chance, now I was hoping it was the last we'd see of the ship.

That blank, empty look in Coen's eyes when he'd stood up on the deck of the *Wellworthy* was burned in my memory. I couldn't shake it. What had that look meant? Did he know that I knew? If he did, what would he do about it?

I hadn't seen him on the ship as I worked for the rest of the day, and I hadn't gone to the tavern because I didn't want to run into any Jevalis looking for payback in Bruin's name. I'd also been hesitant to let Ailee out of my sight, surprising myself with how protective I felt over the girl. The old rules we lived by would have forbidden the risk Ailee had brought into my life, and it was possible I was just filling the empty place West had once occupied. But the thing I feared even more than that reality was the possibility of being alone.

The wind picked up, making the bosun's post groan around me and I smiled to myself, thinking it almost sounded like a ship. Almost. But the smile fell when I heard the creak of wood on the dock outside. I stilled, listening.

A bigger wave crashed against the barrier islands and I relaxed, letting out the breath I was holding. I was skittish, and I didn't like that feeling. It reminded me of those months after Crane, when the burn on my face was healing about as fast as my heart was. I'd been truly terrified, and even more terrified for anyone to know it.

I closed my eyes, trying to push the memories from my mind. I listened to the sound of the water. The wind. The ring of grommets on tilting masts. But my eyes popped back open when I heard a metal click outside the door. No, *at* the door.

My heartbeat quickened as I sat up, silently touching my bare feet to the floor. There were whispers drifting in through the open window. Shadows moving over the wall. Someone was coming.

I stood, reaching into Ailee's hammock to cover her mouth with one hand before I shook her awake with the other. She startled, eyes widening in the dark as they focused on me.

I leaned down, putting my mouth close to her ear.

"Get up," I whispered.

Ailee obeyed, her skinny limbs untangling from the fabric as I helped her to her feet. Another scrape of metal sounded, drawing her gaze to the door, and I could see the moment the panic gripped her. She pushed the curls back from her face, frantically searching the darkness around us.

I pressed a finger to my mouth and pointed to the small window at the back of the post above the counter. It was too small for me, but she could fit. She could get out before that door opened.

Ailee looked from the window to me before shaking her head.

The lock on the door clicked and I went still, watching the flicker of light beneath the door. When I pushed Ailee toward the back window, she planted her feet, refusing again. She didn't relent until I had all but picked her up, hauling her toward it.

I lifted her to the opening and she scrambled through, her black eyes meeting mine for a breath before she melted into the dark. My pulse was a sprint now, my breaths coming so fast that I could feel my head going light. This is how it had been before. That buzz in the air telling me that somewhere terrible was about to happen, only there was nothing I could do to stop it.

My hands fumbled along the wall in search of my belt and when I found it, my fingers hooked the handle of my dagger. My grip closed around it as the door to the post opened, bringing a stream of moonlight inside.

Two silhouettes were painted against the glare and I squared my shoulders to them, my skin going cold as ice. It was Bruin. I'd known it must be, but seeing his shape there against the black sky filled my insides with pure fear. By the time anyone heard me screaming, he'd have his hands around my throat.

"Where's your harbor master now, Willa?" The grin was thick in Bruin's voice.

I lifted the dagger before me, letting my weight shift back and forth from one leg to the other. It was possible I could outrun him, but I'd have to get past him first. That didn't seem likely with two of them. My best chance was to fight like hell and hope I'd bought myself enough time for Ailee to get help.

Bruin took a step toward me and I stood my ground, tightening my grip on the blade. Moonlight glinted off the jewels set into the handle as my hand shook. I could barely keep hold of it.

Bruin waited for three silent, agonizing seconds before he finally charged in my direction, crossing the space so fast that I barely got my dagger through the air before he was knocking me off my feet. The edge of the blade grazed his arm before it slipped from my fingers and the ping of it hitting the floor was the last sound I heard before his fist came down on me.

Bright light erupted in the dark as the blow struck my temple and I cried out, a sob breaking in my chest.

"Help!" I screamed as he jerked me to my feet, and as I drew another breath to scream again, a hand was shoving something into my mouth. A cloth. The bitter taste of tung oil made me gag as he dragged me through the door onto the dock. The other figure stalked behind me as I kicked, desperately reaching out around me for anything I could catch hold of.

The ship decks overhead were dark, the wind covering the sound of the men's footsteps as we passed each slip. Hot tears stung my eyes as the stars in the sky blurred, making me dizzy. No one was coming, I realized. No one was coming for me.

Bruin stopped walking before he hooked his hands beneath my arms and the other man grabbed my feet, lugging me to the edge of the dock. I couldn't see what they were doing, but I could hear it. The clink of chains. The snap of irons as they closed around my ankles.

It hit me all at once what was happening here. He wasn't going to just kill me. He was going to tie me to the reef. Leave me there to drown so the sea creatures could pick my bones clean.

The sound of my scream was muffled in the oil-soaked cloth as I thrashed, nails scratching every surface they could find. Bruin was cursing, pinning me to the dock with all his weight until I couldn't draw breath, and then I heard it. Actually, I could *feel* it.

Footsteps.

The reverberation of a steady beat shook the wooden planks beneath me, but Bruin didn't seem to notice, his focus on the irons. I tilted my head back, but the docks disappeared in the dark, an inky black bleeding through the air as a cloud moved across the face of the moon. It wasn't until the light flickered back that I could see him.

Koy.

Again, I screamed, and Bruin finally looked up, eyes going wide when he saw him.

"Shit."

Frantically, he dragged me closer to the edge and I clawed at the dock, fingers desperately catching each crack in the wood as I slid. But he was too strong. I was going over the edge a second later, and as soon as the splash beneath me sounded, I knew. It was too late.

I saw Koy's face for a split second before the weight began to sink, pulling me under so fast that I barely had time to suck in a breath. I plunged into the cold water, blinking as the salt stung my eyes, and the bubbles raced up in the beams of moonlight that cascaded around me. My hands raked helplessly through the current as the surface drew away from me, and my ears popped before the weight hit the sandy bottom and I halted.

I kicked at the chains, clumsily pulling the cloth from my mouth before I reached down, trying to find the clasp of the iron. He'd only gotten one fastening around my foot, but I couldn't get it free. The opening was just small enough that I couldn't wiggle my heel past it.

Another pathetic cry escaped my lips, sending another stream of bubbles racing up to the surface, and I reached out, hoping I might be close enough to the submerged dock posts to reach. But there was nothing. Only the sound of the waves breaking against the barrier islands and the pounding of my heart.

The light shifted over me, followed by a muted splash, and a figured dropped through the water toward me. Pain bloomed in my chest when I recognized Koy's shape coming closer. He sank past me, pulling at the chains until he'd reached the bottom. Then he was yanking at the iron, trying to wedge my foot out of the loop.

It was no use.

I went still, suspended in the darkness, the glittering pool of light above like a rippling puddle as Koy floated up to meet me. My muscles instantly went weak; every bit of the survival instinct that had been coursing through my veins was gone now, replaced by an inexplicable numb feeling as his hands found my face.

My lungs squeezed, my arms weightless, and the pain left my body the minute I could feel the warmth of his palms. I stopped fighting the gravity tugging at my feet and he pressed his forehead to mine, meeting my eyes. He was waiting for something.

I couldn't make out his face, but suddenly I understood what the tenderness in his touch meant. That moment of silence. My foot wasn't coming out of that iron unless he broke it. It was that or drown.

His fingers grazed over my cheeks, finding my jaw so that he could tilt my face up toward the moonlight. He waited for me to nod, and when I did, I pressed my face into his palm, closing my eyes.

He let me go, pulling himself down again until he had my foot in his hands, and before I could change my mind, his hand wrapped tightly around my ankle. I pinched my eyes closed as the sharp pain dug into the back of my heel, and he didn't stop, prying the metal relentlessly against the bone until that pain was shooting up my leg, into my hip. The moment it cracked, the sound tore through me with a white-hot heat that made me feel like I was on fire inside.

Then I was floating. The lack of air was no longer detectable in my chest. The ache in my ears and throat were gone. I drifted toward the moonlight as my mind all but wiped every single feeling from my body. And when I broke the surface, I gasped, filling my lungs so fast that I was sure they would explode.

Koy came up beside me as I choked and he pulled me alongside him toward the dock, where Ailee was waiting. Bruin and the man were gone, and a few crew from the ships littered the harbor as they watched. Koy's labored breaths were hot against my ear as he pulled me, dead weight, from the water and lifted me into his arms. Then I could hear the sound of his footsteps again, like a heartbeat that brought my own back in line.

I curled into his arms, pressing my face into his neck, and I cried. I wept, a deep, ragged sound breaking me in places I didn't think could crack. His arms tightened around me, holding me to him, and his words were hot against my ear, the only thing I could feel.

"I've got you."

NINE

I woke in Koy's hammock, wrapped in the smell of him.

Sweat dotted my skin everywhere the light touched it, and I turned my face instinctively toward the window, where Koy was leaning into the wall, watching the sea. His gaze was calm, missing the tautness it usually carried, and for a moment, the version of him I first met flashed through my mind. His long, damp hair blown into his face, his black eyes like onyx. He was someone different now. I was, too.

A nearly empty bottle of rye was still cradled in my arms from last night, the pain throbbing between my temples nothing next to the excruciating agony in my foot. It was propped up high, my swollen ankle blackened to a color that turned my stomach when I looked at it. At some point in the night, I remembered being sick and when I spotted the bucket on the floor beneath me, the fuzzy memory resurfaced. I winced, wishing I could erase it.

Koy blinked, eyes finding me, and he immediately left

the window, coming to my side. He took the bottle from my hands, pushing the hair back from my face.

"You slept." He looked down at me, hand stalling on my forehead a beat too long, like he was checking for a fever. "Can you move it?"

Again, I glanced at my foot, cringing. "I don't want to."

"Okay. That's okay."

I turned my face to search the post, looking for Ailee.

"She's checking in with the *Wellworthy*."

"You should be doing that," I croaked, my throat like sand.

"I'm not going anywhere."

"You can't just—" I tried to swallow back the tears springing to my eyes. This was a mess, all of it. "One of us has to be out there, handling things."

"Raef is discharging the ships that are leaving and doing intake for the new ones."

I looked at him. "New ones?"

He nodded. "Two more came in last night."

"I hope they don't need repairs." I pressed a hand to my sweaty forehead.

Any other time, the comment would have been darkly funny. But here, curled in this hammock like a child that needed tending, I was only humiliated. The very thought made the tears spill over and I wiped them with the back of my hand angrily.

"Where's Bruin?" I rasped.

"He's gone."

I didn't look at him, because I didn't want to know exactly

what those words meant. Maybe he'd banished him from the island. Did he have the authority to do that? Or maybe he'd gotten rid of him some other way, like West had done with Crane.

Koy's eyes traveled over me before landing on my foot. His mouth opened and closed before he finally spoke. "I'm sorry, Willa." He breathed. "I had to."

I reached for him, pulling on his shirt until he was close to me. I couldn't bring myself to tell him thank you or tell him that he'd saved my life in more ways than one. I couldn't form the words to say out loud that when I'd seen him on the docks, I'd known I was safe.

"I know I should have listened to you. I should have dealt with them months ago," he said, the words faint.

Maybe he should have, but I wasn't convinced this wouldn't have ended the same. There were those on the island that needed the change, like Speck. Then there were those who would die to prevent it. Jeval was a simmering pot, just waiting to boil over, and it finally had.

"Say it." I smirked through my tears.

When he caught my meaning, he smiled sadly. "You were right."

"I've never heard you say that before."

The tension uncoiled itself from around him and he laughed, a sound I now found myself craving. When my eyes landed on the bundle on the floor behind him, I lifted myself up onto my elbows.

"What is that?"

Koy turned to look at my hammock. It was piled in a heap in the corner.

"You're moving in here," he said, not even an edge of sarcasm in his voice.

"What?"

Koy folded his fingers between mine, turning my hand over to look at my busted knuckles. "You should have done it a long time ago."

So, he did know how I felt about him.

"I wasn't ready," I whispered.

"Well, you are now."

I gave him a brittle smile, the movement making the corner of my lip hurt, and I remembered that my face must be busted, too, after Bruin hit me. I pulled his hand up to where my heart was beating behind my ribs, holding it there. I'd spent so long trying to break free of needing anyone, but the thing was, I didn't *want* to be alone. How long had he known that?

"What about Ailee?" I asked.

"Her, too."

I nodded.

The ring of the bell rang out over the docks, signaling the opening of trade, and almost immediately the harbor came to life outside the window. Shadows flitted over the post as people passed, commands echoing as they were called out on the anchored ships.

Again, I looked at my mangled foot. It would be weeks, if not months, before I could get around on it like I had before. I resisted the urge to ask myself what would happen if I couldn't.

In that time, ships would come and go and other than what we had on hand to trade, Jeval had little to offer beside rye and a place to harbor from a storm.

"We'll have to pull some of the Jevalis who have basic bosun skills and make assignments," I said, thinking aloud. "Ailee and Raef can keep an eye on them and in the meantime, I can work on inventory and plans for the drydock. It won't be a total waste. I promise."

"Willa, a year ago this place didn't even exist. We built it. You and me. I'm not worried."

I smiled again.

The door swung open and a breathless Ailee appeared on the other side, her wild hair flying. She was paler than usual, her dark eyes glinting.

I sat up, instantly regretting it when the pain shot through my leg. "What's wrong?"

"The *Wellworthy*."

I stilled. "What about it?"

"It's—it's gone," she stammered.

"What do you mean it's gone?" My voice rose.

Ailee wrung her hands. "Some of the crew from the *Iris* said it raised its sails well before dawn. When the sun came up, they were already west on the horizon."

My brow pulled. "West? I thought they were headed to Sowan next."

"That's what the navigator told me," Koy said.

I stared at him, putting it together slowly. "I wasn't even finished sealing the wood, Koy."

Understanding settled between us.

"The only reason the *Wellworthy* could possibly have for leaving without discharge from the harbor master and with no notice at all is because they are running," I said.

"But from what?"

That was the thing. I had my suspicions about Coen being responsible for the death of the deckhand from Sowan, but there was no evidence. Nothing linking him to what happened. What was the urgency?

"Or." A sick feeling pooled in my stomach. "Maybe they weren't running *from* something, but *to* something."

Ailee's eyes jumped back and forth between us.

"Koy," I panted, "if Coen did hear what I heard that night . . ."

"He's headed to the Unnamed Sea," he finished my thought. There was a hollow silence for several seconds before he finally spoke again. This time, it was to Ailee. "Get up to bay one. Tell the *Featherback* to wait."

Ailee nodded, turning on her heel, and then she was gone.

"What? Why?"

"It's too dangerous to send a letter. You're going to Ceros yourself."

I was struggling to sit up now, gasping as I lowered my damaged foot from the hammock. "What the hell are you talking about?" I ground out.

Koy didn't meet my eyes. He went to the counter at the back of the post, taking a purse of copper from the shelf and lifting something from one of the hooks on the wall. It took me a moment to realize it was my belt. My dagger was safely fastened in its sheath.

"The *Featherback* is headed straight there. We'll pay for passage. West should be there in a week at most, right?"

"Yeah, but . . ."

"But what?"

I couldn't find the words, my eyes fixing on his as a storm of thoughts swirled in my head. Only last night I'd nearly died, and now the last thing I wanted to do was leave.

"I can't just go."

"You need a physician anyway, Willa."

"But," I said the useless word again, though I didn't know what came after it.

Koy draped my jacket over his arm, holding out a hand to help me stand. "You'll come back," he said, sifting out the root of this panic that was overtaking me.

A flood of relief filled me, as if I'd just needed one of us to say it out loud. I nodded and he smiled before he pressed his lips to mine. For the first time. He drew in a long, slow breath as he kissed me, making that fire in my chest spill over. It pulled me out to sea.

When his mouth broke from mine, he was still smiling, and the tears were back in my eyes without my permission. I wrapped my arms around his neck and he lifted me the way he had last night, careful not to hit my foot as he ducked out the door of the post. Over his shoulder, I scanned the harbor, counting each bay in my head, the way I did every morning.

"Don't let Ailee work on any ships alone. And don't take

on repairs unless you know we can fix it," I said, mind racing. "Make sure you take at least half the payment up front."

"I know."

"And don't—"

"Willa, I know," he said again.

"What's all this, Koy?" A voice called down from the *Featherback* and I looked up to see the helmsman peering over the railing.

"Passage. She needs a physician," he called out. "We can pay."

The helmsman's mustache twitched. "Well, of course." He motioned in the air. "Get the sling down there!"

A moment later, the lines were lowering and I was hoisting myself into them. "I have about as good a chance making it there as I do sinking with this rotten ship," I muttered. "Look after Ailee."

Koy nodded.

"I mean it," I said, a quiet desperation surfacing in my voice.

His hand squeezed mine. "I will."

The ropes creaked as they tightened and he kissed my fingers as the crew lifted me into the air. Then hands were gently pulling me over the railing onto the deck. Beside Koy, Ailee was watching me with wide eyes. I could have sworn I saw her lip quivering.

The sails snapped as the wind caught them and the ship drifted from the dock, slipping into the current. They were all growing smaller by the second. Koy, Ailee, the harbor, the island. A rush of cold dread slowly took shape inside of me, my mind spinning around one single thought.

I was headed back to the *Marigold,* but for the first time, it didn't feel like going home.

ABOUT THE AUTHOR

ADRIENNE YOUNG is a foodie with a deep love of history and travel and a shameless addiction to coffee. When she's not writing, you can find her on her yoga mat, sipping wine over long dinners or disappearing into her favorite art museums. She lives with her documentary filmmaker husband and their four little wildlings in the Blue Ridge Mountains of North Carolina. She is the author of the *New York Times* bestselling *Sky in the Deep* duology and the *Fable* duology. She posts on Instagram @adrienneyoungbooks.

NAMESAKE

BY ADRIENNE YOUNG

Trader. Fighter. Legend.

With the *Marigold* ship free of her father, Fable and its crew were set to start over. That freedom is short-lived when she becomes a pawn in a notorious thug's scheme. In order to get to her intended destination she must help him to secure a partnership with Holland, a powerful gem trader who is more than she seems.

As Fable descends deeper into a world of betrayal and deception, she learns that the secrets her mother took to her grave are now putting the people Fable cares about in danger. If Fable is going to save them then she must risk everything, including the boy she loves and the home she has finally found.

"An exciting, fast-paced ride that will ultimately satisfy those that stepped on board the Marigold with Fable last year...There's plenty to love about this sequel: Its relentless pace keeps the story feeling as though something new and dramatic is happening on every page."

— CULTURESS

TITANBOOKS.COM

For more fantastic fiction, author events,
exclusive excerpts, competitions, limited editions and more

VISIT OUR WEBSITE
titanbooks.com

LIKE US ON FACEBOOK
facebook.com/titanbooks

FOLLOW US ON TWITTER AND INSTAGRAM
@TitanBooks

EMAIL US
readerfeedback@titanemail.com